The Information Brokers' Gossip

"Did you hear what the 'classified you-know-whos' have been up to lately?"

"Yes, Nicholas and Elean were talking about it. You mean the one about Huey Laforet and...Vino teaming up, right? Henry looked like he'd seen a ghost."

"Well, Vino almost killed the guy once."

"Served him right."

"That aside, how do you think this is gonna go? I mean, come on. An immortal terrorist has the most dangerous hitman who ever lived in his pocket."

"This is Vino, remember? Do you really think he'd let anyone push him around? Rachel says that fella wouldn't take orders from the president of the United States without a fight."

"Well, maybe they think they're using each other. Vino might be after immortality, too."

"Don't even say it. If that hitman was immortal, nobody could stop him."

"Conversely, if Huey genuinely has Vino at his beck and call now..."

"Like I said, knock it off. Huey really would take over the country if that were true."

"Even if it's just a crazy rumor, let's say he did end up with the nation in the palm of his hand. What do you figure would happen to us?"

"Well, probably nothing. I bet he'd just keep treating everybody as his guinea pigs. Whether he's a terrorist or a dictator, that's not gonna change."

"...What do you think they're after? Both of 'em, Huey and Vino."

"Search me. I may be an information broker, but I'm no mind reader.

"All I can say is...it definitely won't end well."

"Hee-hee! Hey, bro, tell me another one. Somethin' about Ladd and Graham. Those guys are somethin' else."

"What's wrong with you? Don't hero-worship those loons! I tell you those stories so you'll know to stay away from 'em, genius!"

"B-but they ain't here in town no more, right?"

"...Yeah, and that's one hell of a relief. When they were hanging around, I felt like a dead man walking, no lie."

"Did they work you over, too?"

"Like hell. You think I'm stupid?"

"I—I dunno. Sorry, man. Are you?"

"...Ah, forget it. Those two are bad news together, but they're even worse separately."

"Huh? Ain't that usually the other way around?"

The Chicago Thugs' Gossip

"Not in this case, it ain't! If you're gonna run into 'em, you want 'em together! Listen up. Both that psycho killer and that whack-job wrecker are bad news, both their brains and their brawn, and the only one who can stop 'em if they go off the rails is the other one! If Graham cuts loose, Ladd stops him after a while; if Ladd seems liable to start butchering everybody for no reason, Graham steps in. That balance is why we ain't dead!"

"...Then, hey, so what if both those guys snap at once?"

"I've never seen it happen, but..."

"But what?"

"I bet any poor bastards nearby would find themselves in one hell of a tornado."

"Good thing they ain't in Chicago no more, huh."

"Yep, and that's why I'm stayin' here till further notice.

"Unless those freaks come back, that is."

The Wealthy's Gossip

"I swear, will this recession never end?"

"It's truly dire. I had assets in reserve, fortunately, but there's no telling how many more years this may drag on."

"Well, let's hope our president can pull through. May the lights of Millionaires' Row never go out, even in these dark times."

"...Still, I can already see the effects of the Depression here. I've spotted some strange, thuggish characters on the Avenue in the past few years."

"Oh, I imagine that was the housekeeping staff from Miss Genoard's second residence."

"Staff? They didn't look like anything of the sort..."

"Yes, I was concerned myself at first. I had no idea what was going on. Miss Genoard's father and older brother have passed away, and the young lady has inherited the family. She's a woman of outstanding virtue, but I was concerned that scoundrels had taken advantage of her kindness."

"But you say that isn't the case?"

"On one occasion, I observed those odd housekeepers very closely. There are young children in that group, and their smiles were so very innocent. At the very least, we can be sure they wouldn't harm children."

"Then it really is all right?"

"Well, mind you, there have been a few strange disturbances. Still, when I spoke to their leader—the young man with the tattoo on his face—he was a very pleasant fellow."

"Oh, you must be joking. He has a tattoo! On his face!"

"No, no, he was quite an entertaining character. I imagine that's the side of him Miss Eve saw.

"...Although, really, anyone would look positively virtuous next to that middle child. The lout's left the family to his sister, and he does nothing but fritter his days and his money away."

"Hey, what's up with that new fella—Melvin or Melface or whatever the hell his name is?"

"Melvi? I dunno much about him, either, but they say he's the new dealer. He'll be on-site running the gambling during the casino opening."

"That's nuts! A big event like the debut, and they're leaving it to a newbie? Who is he anyway? Which gambling den did he work at and where?"

"Well, that's the thing—apparently, he's not one of our guys, period."

"...What? So he's an outsider?"

"Yeah. Remember that terrorist Mr. Runorata's been hiding lately? Huey Laforet? He's the one who brought him in."

"What the hell? How does a guy like that suddenly get handed a major job?"

"Well, Laforet's wanted by the BOI, see... Whoops, I think they're keepin' the whole prison-break story under wraps. Anyway, he's one hell of a terrorist, and he went out of his way to introduce the kid to us. He's gotta have something good."

"I don't like it. If we put this schmuck in charge, what's gonna happen to the family's rep?"

"Hey."

"...Wh-what? Why're you glaring at me?"

"Those orders came from Mr. Runorata himself. If you got a problem, take it straight to him. If all you can do is grouse, then the Runorata Family won't need any outside help losing its reputation."

"O-okay already. Geez, what? So you trust that punk, too?"

"I just respect the boss's decision, as a member of the family. Personally, I think he's fishy.

"Even fishier than Huey."

Design: Yoshihiko Kamabe

BACCANO!

1935-B Dr. Feelgreed

VOLUME 19

RYOHGO NARITA
ILLUSTRATION BY KATSUMI ENAMI

YEN ON

NEW YORK

BACCANO!, Volume 19: 1935-B DR. FEELGREED
RYOHGO NARITA

Translation by Taylor Engel
Yen On edition edited by Carly Smith & Anna Powers
Cover art by Katsumi Enami

BACCANO! Vol.19
©Ryohgo Narita 2012
Edited by Dengeki Bunko
First published in Japan in 2012 by KADOKAWA CORPORATION, Tokyo.
English translation rights arranged with KADOKAWA CORPORATION, Tokyo,
through Tuttle-Mori Agency, Inc., Tokyo.

English translation © 2022 by Yen Press, LLC

Yen On
150 West 30th Street, 19th Floor
New York, NY 10001

Visit us at yenpress.com
facebook.com/yenpress
twitter.com/yenpress
yenpress.tumblr.com
instagram.com/yenpress

First Yen On Edition: May 2022

Yen On is an imprint of Yen Press, LLC.
The Yen On name and logo are trademarks of Yen Press, LLC.

Library of Congress Cataloging-in-Publication Data
Names: Narita, Ryōgo, 1980– author. | Engel, Taylor, translator.
Title: Baccano! / Ryohgo Narita ; translation by Taylor Engel.
Description: First Yen On edition. | New York : Yen On, 2016–
Identifiers: LCCN 2015045300 | ISBN 9780316270366 (v. 1 : hardback) |
ISBN 9780316270397 (v. 2 : hardback) | ISBN 9780316270410 (v. 3 : hardback) |
ISBN 9780316270434 (v. 4 : hardback) | ISBN 9780316558662 (v. 5 : hardback) |
ISBN 9780316442275 (v. 6 : hardback) | ISBN 9780316442312 (v. 7 : hardback) |
ISBN 9780316442329 (v. 8 : hardback) | ISBN 9780316442343 (v. 9 : hardback) |
ISBN 9780316442367 (v. 10 : hardback) | ISBN 9781975356859 (v. 11 : hardback) |
ISBN 9781975384715 (v. 12 : hardback) | ISBN 9781975384739 (v. 13 : hardback) |
ISBN 9781975384753 (v. 14 : hardback) | ISBN 9781975384777 (v. 15 : hardback) |
ISBN 9781975321567 (v. 16 : hardback) | ISBN 9781975321901 (v. 17 : hardback) |
ISBN 9781975321925 (v. 18 : hardback) | ISBN 9781975321949 (v. 19 : hardback)
Subjects: CYAC: Science fiction. | Nineteen twenties—Fiction. | Organized crime—Fiction. |
Prohibition—Fiction. | BISAC: FICTION / Science Fiction / Adventure.
Classification: LCC PZ7.1.N37 Bac 2016 | DDC [Fic]—dc23
LC record available at http://lccn.loc.gov/2015045300

ISBNs: 978-1-9753-2194-9 (hardcover)
978-1-9753-2195-6 (ebook)

1 3 5 7 9 10 8 6 4 2

LSC-C

Printed in the United States of America

All right, Huey Laforet. Let's get this show on the road.

This time, there's no friend to shut down your rampage.
Let yourself go, expose your greed, and stew in your own arrogance.

Naturally…there's no friend to save you, either.
Yes, that creepy smile junkie isn't in town. Isn't that wonderful?
You won't have to worry about letting him see
your shameful behavior.

And I won't have to see his detestable face.

Linking Chapter   **Can't Fight the Current**

Somewhere in New York   A casino

The situation could be summed up in one simple word: *chaos*.

An eerie feeling had seized Firo Prochainezo, Martillo Family executive—as if his heart had been caught in layer upon layer of spiderwebs.

It was the first time in his twenty-odd years that he'd found himself in such confused circumstances, and his mind couldn't keep up with the reality in front of him.

That said, he was resilient enough to become a Camorra executive at a young age, so maybe that was why he kept working to understand the situation at all.

If Firo's life were a vast ocean, it would have a few whirlpools in it. Becoming a member of the Martillo Family had given him a current that pushed him forward in his life; however, becoming an immortal had pulled him into a huge vortex between the ocean currents.

Firo had been caught in this whirlpool for several years, but a few months earlier, his involuntary trip to Alcatraz had sucked him in even deeper.

Events today had dragged him right to its heart: a casino breaker; a man who'd apparently won on the slots by cheating; visits from Ladd Russo and Christopher; Maiza Avaro, his boss and a senior immortal; and a dead ringer for Maiza's kid brother, Gretto, who had arrived and declared himself Firo's enemy.

All of this on its own might have been enough to drag him into the maelstrom, but Maiza had told him something else that served as the final push.

"There are airplanes outside...? What are you talking about, Maiza?" Firo replied, confused.

Maiza calmly explained that multiple fighter planes had appeared in the sky over New York and were firing machine guns mounted on them. The city didn't seem to be taking any damage, so he assumed they were probably firing blanks.

In that moment, another whirlpool was added to Firo's life, and his mind almost stopped in the chaos.

He didn't panic, though. His obligations and pride as a Martillo Family executive, plus the presence of two other executives he loved and respected, kept him anchored to sanity.

If he'd succumbed to the urge to scream and smash whatever he could, he might have felt a little better, but that wouldn't fix the situation.

Firo had realized if he sank into that whirlpool right now, he'd drag down people who were important to him, too.

"Maiza, you don't look so great. You okay?" Firo asked, partly to help himself calm down.

"I don't?" Maiza said, startled by the observation. "Oh, well, it's true that I'm confused. It isn't only the situation outside. Just now, I passed someone who bore a strong resemblance to an acquaintance of mine..."

"Yeah. *I know.*" Firo nodded firmly, and with that, Maiza was caught in a whirlpool of his own. He'd wanted to write it off as a chance resemblance, but under the circumstances, he couldn't bring himself to say it.

"...What was he? I do know he can't be...*him,*" Maiza said.

"Oh, uh, it'll take a while to fill you in on the details, but… The short version is, he's with the Runorata Family."

"The Runoratas…?" Maiza's eyebrows drew together.

Someone else interrupted them. "That conversation can wait until after we've dealt with the casino."

"Ronny."

Like Maiza, Ronny Schiatto was a senior executive.

At the phrase "dealt with the casino," Firo took another look around the room. "For now…I'll have the kids work on cleaning the place up. It's not like all the tables are broken, so if everything goes well, we'll be able to open again tomorrow."

Ladd Russo had been listening in, and now he spoke up. He was one of the people who'd trashed the casino. "Seriously, Firo, sorry about that. If you want, I'll get you some replacement tables by tomorrow."

"I ain't usin' any tables you brought in. Not worth the risk."

"Cautious fella. Well, that ain't a bad thing… By the way, who're these guys? Introduce me, wouldja?" Ladd smiled at Ronny and Maiza. Firo froze.

"Yes, Firo, who are they?" Maiza asked, motioning toward Ladd and Graham, but Firo wouldn't look at either of them.

"Uh, I'll introduce you later. You too, Ladd. Just sit tight, all right?"

After Firo had put them off for the moment, a question occurred to him. Now that all their customers had scattered, he saw faces that didn't look like they belonged in a casino.

What's Christopher doing here anyway? Who are the two kids he's got with him? Wait, one of those kids has some crazy scars.

Now was probably not the time to ask those questions, but to settle his mind, he decided to start somewhere. Although he'd said he'd introduce everyone later, would it be better to get Maiza, Ladd, and the rest acquainted now?

No, wait. Those kids might be outsiders. I get the feeling they came in with Ronny, though…

He decided he'd better check on that with the man himself. "By the way, Ronny, are those people acquaintances of—? Hmm?" His eyes fell on a certain face, and he broke off.

"Eeep?!" a tattooed kid shrieked as Firo's gaze stopped on him. He was standing next to Ronny, and Firo kept staring.

"Hey… I think I recognize that tattoo," Firo said.

"Aaaah! I—I'msorryexcusemeforgiveme!" the boy shrieked all in a rush.

With that, the tattooed newcomer was dragged into a new whirlpool.

Although this particular boy—Jacuzzi Splot—had already been on the verge of drowning in a maelstrom of his own.

And so the story picked up speed.

Firo Prochainezo's whirlpool was the trouble around the casino. That said, history's great ocean was shared property. The people around Firo were being dragged into their own separate vortices. The whirlpools of their lives overlapped, and nobody could predict where the currents would take them anymore.

What lay in their hearts? Did the same thing lie beneath every one of the maelstroms?

They simply continued drifting through life, unable to catch so much as a glimpse of the bottom.

Should they escape from the whirlpools? Or should they give in to them and peer into their depths?

They didn't know the answers to even these basic questions.

At this point, all they could do was let the massive current carry them along.

Digression 2 The Sweetheart Is Guileless

2003   Dalton, library director and immortal, speaks of the past

Let me tell you an old story.

As you probably know, I was once an alchemist. I may still be one, but my main job is "library director."

How do I hide my identity from those around me? Oh, there are any number of ways to do that. I don't mind describing them in detail, but this particular story already promises to be a long one, so we'll save that for another time.

However, even now that I've become immortal—now that I'm no longer human—I've remained an alchemist. It's a funny thing.

Has becoming immortal brought me fortune or misfortune? I've pondered that question many times, but to be honest with you, I don't know.

As an Eastern proverb says, "Good fortune and bad alternate like the strands of a rope." I've experienced my share of both fortune and misfortune as an immortal.

If you asked ordinary people, "Was your life a happy one?", unless you posed your question just before they died, no doubt most wouldn't have an answer immediately ready for you. Also, naturally, the conclusion would vary depending on the individual. That's true for immortals as well. After all, the balance of fortune and misfortune is different for everyone.

Let's see…

While it didn't register as happiness in the moment, in retrospect, I have had many experiences that I can categorically declare were happy ones.

When I first became immortal, I spent a while traveling around the world.

I and the apprentices from my studio strove to plumb the depths of a variety of fields. However, our efforts to reach their true essence were hampered by our lack of knowledge and experience, and most of all…by our overwhelming lack of time.

When my acquaintance Battuta told me of the elixir of immortality, I initially thought she was teasing me. But from the moment she showed me what it meant to be an immortal, I was captivated.

For some alchemists, immortality is their original goal. In my case, it was a means to an end. If I were immortal, I would gain unlimited time. Even if experiments took a century or a millennium to show results, I could see them to completion with my own eyes. Those were my genuine feelings on the matter.

After all, my hair and whiskers were already as white as they are now.

The thought of dying and returning to oblivion held no particular terror for me. It was only that I didn't want to contemplate the thought of breaking off my research before it was finished, of being unable to see the outcome.

Consequently, I and nine of my apprentices summoned a demon and became immortals.

At this point, the idea of alchemists summoning demons sounds ludicrous. However, there was a time when alchemy was viewed in the same light as devil worship and mysticism, and there were some who made no distinction between us and magicians.

Once immortal, over the next five hundred years, I saw all sorts of things.

At first, it was painful to watch my ordinary acquaintances die one after another, but I gradually grew accustomed to it. I am told that many who became immortal in the past were unable to come to terms with it and summoned the demon once more to kill—or "eat"—them. Though none of my apprentices did so, at the very least.

Yes, over those long years, I saw many, many things.

Wise rulers and tyrants, transformational moments in the very workings of society—everything from practical matters to the grotesques that lurk in the shadows of the world. You may not believe me, but on an island in the north, I even saw werewolves and vampires. As you can imagine, I thought I might have been dreaming the time I saw several shadowy headless knights on horseback in Ireland, riding in formation. No, that may actually have been a dream...

At any rate, whenever I saw something I had never seen before, it felt as though the very world had expanded. It exhilarated me far too much for one of my years.

Looking back, I really was content then.

Conversely...my unhappiest time was when I lost most of my apprentices.

Originally, I ran an alchemy studio in Northern Europe. A moment ago, I said I'd had nine apprentices. Including myself, all ten of us became immortals.

To be honest, only three of us are left.

Yes, yes, you're right. Earlier, I said that none had chosen to end their own lives by asking the demon to eat them. Nor were they consumed by someone who'd become immortal on some other occasion.

It was us.

Our companions ate one another.

The first ten years were peaceful—and I realize now that may have been a miracle.

It started with one timid apprentice's suspicion and desire to defend himself.

Now that no mere illness or injury would kill us, the one thing that could act as our death-scythe was another immortal's right hand, and that man had an excessive fear of them.

It's a comical story.

"I don't want to die, not after I've become immortal." It's laughable, but that was what my apprentice thought, and to escape that fear… he ate another apprentice. His own mother, of all people.

From that point on, everything happened in the blink of an eye. Rather, that's how it felt to me. After all, the killing went on for three years.

The motives varied. Some felt paranoia, like that first apprentice, while others were possessed by greed. Still, others simply ate and called it an experiment.

At the end of this ugly cannibalism, the only ones left were myself, Renee, and…a man named Archangelo.

Renee is a brilliant alchemist but rather lacking as a human being. The girl has no concept of danger.

How did she survive, you ask? It's simple: She was protected. By myself, I wish I could say, but that wasn't the case. While my apprentices were consuming one another, I threw myself into my research so I wouldn't have to face reality.

You could say that man was far better than I was, for whatever it's worth. Archangelo protected Renee to the end, and his motive for consuming others was love… That's really all it was.

Archangelo was fond of Renee. To protect her from the right hands of his fellow apprentices, he ate all the survivors. He was a faithful man. At the very least, he wasn't a villain. He was straitlaced, like an unbribable civil servant. Maybe it was his serious side that made it impossible for him to choose a different path from mine.

Nonetheless, even after he'd done all that, he still didn't confess his love to Renee. It wasn't due to inexperience; he knew full well what the result would be.

Renee Parmedes Branvillier isn't capable of understanding love from others. She isn't human enough.

Lacking… Yes, she is lacking in humanity. Maybe she was born that way, or perhaps it's the result of trauma—I don't know. She was like that by the time she became my apprentice.

Archangelo knew his love for Renee would never be reciprocated. He was also aware that he would hinder her work as a researcher. As a result, he continued to protect her while keeping a slight distance between them—and before he knew it, he'd ended up eating many of the other apprentices.

He turned suspicious eyes on me as well, but I categorically refused to be eaten for a reason like that. I made a deal with him.

That's why my right hand is a prosthetic.

As you know, if those who've drunk the elixir of immortality want to kill each other, they need their right hands.

I cut off my own right hand, and as it tried to return to my wrist, I pinned it to a board with my knife. When I held out my arm to Archangelo, he looked bewildered. Yes, it's a rare occurrence for him. In any case, I gave him my right hand and had him seal it in a place only he knows.

I did it to prove I wasn't his enemy.

I wasn't frightened of him. I was just fed up with my apprentices killing one another. You could definitely say I was unhappy then.

Perhaps it means that, unlike Renee, I still had some human emotions left.

…Or possibly I was just sad that I had fewer assistants to help with my experiments.

At this point, there's no way to tell which it was. There's also no need to.

After all, no matter how things may have been in the past, that incident cost me most of my humanity.

Don't you see? If I'd had any humanity left, why would I have gone out of my way to make others immortal?

There were several reasons I taught Maiza Avaro how to summon the demon.

…Although I've forgotten most of them, by now.

Ah yes, when you become an immortal, the capacity of your

memory does increase, as compared to ordinary humans. When I forget anything, it happens in the usual way. However, from the fact that I've lived several centuries and my memory hasn't imploded on me, the true form of our immortality itself really must be…

Whoops, I almost wasted our time on a different tale. My apologies. Steel yourself; the old tell long stories.

At any rate, I gave Maiza a path to immortality in the full knowledge that he and the rest might begin to kill one another. I don't know whether what I did brought misfortune to my new apprentices: Maiza, Elmer, and Huey. No doubt it will take several centuries, or millennia, to know the results of that.

You could say it's an experiment made possible by immortality.

An experiment… Yes, one could call what I did to Maiza's group an experiment. My actions amounted to using my beloved apprentices as guinea pigs.

…Do you think me a brute?

In that case, you're still normal. If you can avoid it, you shouldn't get involved with this grotesque world.

I pray you'll find happiness as an ordinary human.

Mind you, I don't know what that looks like for you, and I won't burden myself to find out.

Chapter 8   The Immortal Researcher Isn't Shy

1935   Chicago

"Hey, any luck?"

"No, she's not here. Several of her personal items are gone, too."

A few men and women in white lab coats were scrambling around inside an orderly lab. It was housed in the headquarters of Nebula, one of America's leading conglomerates. This was a section with even more secrets than the new product development division: a research facility focused on the immortals.

The members of the research team were running this way and that through its corridors, their faces pale.

"Not good. So, what, she's 'gone out' for real this time?"

"Once she does that, she stays out for half a year."

The researchers grumbled, grimacing and patently fed up.

"She's already made one hell of a mess. What's she going to do in *that* state?" one man said, not bothering to hide his anxious irritation.

Another researcher came rushing in. "She left a letter!"

"Where?!"

"Um…at the main reception desk… The clerk was confused; he said he didn't know what it was for."

"Why'd she leave it there?!" The researchers were about to start pulling their hair out, firing questions at the messenger.

"Still, I'm impressed you managed to find it. Did she write the department's name on it or something?"

"No, it was, uh…" The man faltered, and then an elderly fellow with a surprisingly youthful comportment poked his head out from behind him.

"Well, y'see, the letter was originally addressed to me."

"Ch-Chairman?!"

The newcomer was unmistakably Cal Muybridge: chairman of Nebula and the wealthiest, most powerful man in the building. Although age had deepened the hollows of his face, he was smiling like a mischievous kid.

"But y'know, when I read it, well, it was somethin' youse needed to know. So I brought it over here myself. This place technically deals in classified info, so I couldn't just hand the job off to somebody else, see?"

The chairman spoke to them candidly in a heavy Chicago accent, but the researchers' expressions stayed tense.

Renee Parmedes Branvillier, research director and the person responsible for this department, had *disappeared*.

It was a complete disgrace.

The researchers were Renee's subordinates, but they were also her "guards."

While her knowledge as an immortal and her skills as a scientist were excellent, when it came to the rest of life, she had a few screws loose. You could have said she was missing several, in fact, and the ones she lacked were generally critical to survival as a human. In addition, she was much sillier than the average person, and she tripped over absolutely nothing and fell practically every day.

The researchers were responsible for keeping an eye on her to make sure she didn't do anything too crazy or inadvertently blurt out classified information, and this time they'd failed. Renee had vanished so unexpectedly that they hadn't even seen any warning signs.

She'd disappeared a few times before, and even the chairman didn't know what she'd done while she was gone. They could have tried to torture it out of her, but as a complete immortal, she outranked them; the researchers were incomplete immortals, no more than prey. Keeping her restrained for years would end up delaying their research for just as long, so in the end, all Nebula could do was observe her.

That said, Cal found Renee quite entertaining.

"So here's that letter." Cal handed an envelope from his jacket to the researchers, who accepted it deferentially. One opened it and took out a single sheet of stationery.

In the next moment, they were all struck dumb.

The contents of the letter were extremely simple, and that only made their confusion worse.

I'm sorry, Chairman. I'm going to go see my children and students for the first time in ages, so I'll be away for a few days, or maybe a few weeks. (Or a few months?) Anyway, please cover for me with everybody at the lab so they don't get angry. Thank you. Don't worry about paying me for the time I'm gone!

"……"

For a while, the researchers were speechless.

"What the hell?" one of them muttered. Once the silence was broken, everyone started to let out their grievances at once.

"I don't understand a word of this. Children?! Did the director have kids?!"

"Who's she married to?!"

"What's this business about students?!"

"'Don't worry about paying me for the time I'm gone.' That goes without saying! Why does she sound so holier-than-thou?! And hey, Director, normally you'd get fired for this stunt!"

"I guess all the nutrients that should have gone to her brain really did go to her boobs…"

"That's it." "That's the one." "Put me down for that."

"And Director Renee's got a husband… Lucky jerk…"

Somewhere in the middle, the complaints had begun to veer off in another direction. Chairman Cal listened with a smile. When it sounded as though they'd gotten the worst of it out of their systems, he clapped his hands, pulling their attention to himself. "Okay, okay, so do youse get what's goin' on now?"

"Chairman…"

"In that case, let's go with this. Let's say Miz Renee is flyin' over to England 'cause I asked her to. Sound good?"

"…Sir?"

The researchers didn't understand. They weren't sure how to answer.

Cal looked at them, sighed, and elaborated. "I mean, it says it right there in the letter. Uhhh, yeah, right there. 'Please cover for me with everybody at the lab so they don't get angry.' That bit."

"Uh-huh…"

"So *I just covered for her with you.* I said she's gone to England."

"Huh?" Finally realizing what the chairman was getting at, the researchers looked from him to the letter and back again.

"So that means we're all done here. My sneaky white lie left youse none the wiser, ready to return to your duties without worryin' about Miz Renee. When she gets back, nobody's gonna say a word. Right?"

"Huh? No, um…"

The researchers exchanged looks, wondering what the old guy was talking about.

"Right?"

Still smiling, Cal narrowed his eyes, prompting them again, and any breath that might have left their mouths was nervously sucked back into their lungs.

The man's words had had an intimidating, freezing edge.

Suddenly, the researchers remembered that although Cal Muybridge had been talking to them in a folksy way, this old guy wasn't a figurehead chairman or a body double. He was the giant who had built Nebula, this enormous corporation, in a single generation.

"R-right... Director Renee is in England."

"I'm, uh... I'm hopin' she brings us back a nice gift!"

Wearing strained smiles, the researchers nodded to one another. Seeing this, Cal gave a satisfied nod of his own, letting the pressure evaporate. "You betcha. I hope she brings us back somethin' that's kinda, well, sexy. It is Renee, after all." With a leering laugh, the chairman gave a little wave and left.

When the back of the corporation's ultimate authority had disappeared through the door, the researchers all exhaled at once. Then they took another look at the letter and scowled at their direct supervisor, who was at the center of all this.

"...What in the world is Director Renee up to and where?

"She hasn't adjusted to that missing eye yet, and she's tripping and falling more than ever..."

⇔

Meanwhile　　On a train

The transcontinental railroad ran all across America.

On a train from Chicago to New York, there was a woman with too much time on her hands in a first-class compartment.

"La-da-dum-de-duuum. ♪"

She was swinging her dangling legs one by one in time with the tune she was humming.

She seemed to be taking a freewheeling trip by herself, but there was something a little odd about her; beneath her glasses, one of her eyes was clearly false.

That eye had been *stolen* during a certain incident, and she'd fitted an original prosthetic into the empty socket. In lieu of a pupil, the eye had a drawing of a famous animal character from the talkies, which made for a rather off-putting first impression. However, the woman's laid-back attitude canceled out the strangeness.

Wild, majestic scenery and townscapes flowed past the window, but the woman seemed to have gotten bored with them. Her gaze wandered aimlessly around the compartment.

"Dum-da-da-daaah. Da-daaaa-dah. Da-du-du-duuuum. ♪"

At first, she'd thought up random tunes to hum, but that had gotten to be too much trouble, and she began humming scales instead.

Just then, her tedium was interrupted by a rhythmic knock.

"Yes, yes. I'm in here." The woman broke off her humming and gave a rather off-kilter response.

The man outside the compartment didn't sound the least bit confused. "I see. I understand that you're inside. Now, may I come in?"

"Huh? Ummm... That voice, the way you talk... I know! You're Elmer, aren't you?!"

"No."

"What?!"

Ignoring the woman's surprise, the man opened the compartment door with a rattle and looked in.

He wore a bowler hat, pulled down low. For some reason, the hat was snugly secured to his head with a chin strap. He was still young, but there was a strange hardness about him that made him seem middle-aged.

At the sight of him, the woman clapped her hands together in recognition. "Oh, if it isn't Archangelo! Goodness, you startled me! Is it that much fun to surprise little old me?"

The woman didn't sound startled at all. Archangelo heaved a sigh, his face expressionless, then spoke her name. "Renee, please explain what on earth made you mistake me for your student Elmer."

"Huh? I just assumed Elmer was imitating you... I thought it would be boring if you just showed up in the usual way."

"I apologize for being uninteresting, but I've come to discuss something even duller."

"Oh, have you? Ah, do sit down, please."

The woman—Renee Parmedes Branvillier—glanced at the compartment's empty seats. Archangelo closed the door before slowly lowering himself into one of them.

She'd left her company and boarded a train in strict secrecy, so how had he ended up on the same train? The question *never even occurred to her.* She wasn't flustered at all by it. She simply switched roles from speaker to listener.

"Renee. There is something in your actions over these past few decades that warrants a direct rebuke."

"Y-yes? What might that be...? Um, Archangelo, you always look so scary. Smile a little more, okay?"

"Please don't speak like Elmer. That said, if you would look at me amorously, I would not be entirely averse to smiling."

"Erm, well... Your face is kind of scary, so I don't want to."

Their conversation had circled right back. Archangelo cleared his throat lightly, then confronted her without mercy or pity. "Renee, what exactly are you doing? First you push young Miss Niki onto Lady Lucrezia and abruptly cross to the New World. Then you join forces with a corporation and make a veritable horde of people research immortality." His tone was sharp but not overly cruel.

Renee cocked her head. "...Um, why ask me a question you already know the answer to?"

"?"

"What am I doing? You just told me: I put Niki in Lucrezia's care and have been researching immortality with lots of Nebula's employees."

"......" The conversation was going nowhere. Archangelo sighed, pinching the bridge of his nose. "Let me rephrase. *Why* are you doing these things?"

"Why...? Because I thought it might accelerate my research. Oh, are you worried that word about the immortals might spread? I don't think that concern is warranted. Unlike me, the people at Nebula can keep secrets, and I've gone around muzzling people and making backroom deals."

When he heard that, Archangelo looked down. His eyes held a tinge of sadness. "You haven't changed, Renee." He kept the emotion from his voice, though, as she spoke of the past as if it wasn't personal. "It has been several centuries since you became immortal along with Professor Dalton and myself, but your mind is still missing several important faculties. In fact, one might say that becoming immortal has removed the very need to compensate for those missing pieces."

"What are you talking about?"

Renee wasn't playing dumb. She genuinely didn't understand what Archangelo was getting at.

Slowly, the immortal youth got to his feet. Then he placed his *right hand* on Renee's head. Anyone who had obtained the elixir of immortality with the demon's help would know instantly what that meant. It was how immortals "ate" each other.

However, Renee only looked up at the man, blinking in confusion. "What's the matter, Archangelo?"

"……"

He stayed frozen in that position for a little while. Then he withdrew his right hand, his expression still hard. "You truly haven't changed. Your complete disregard for yourself, even after all these years, is genuinely impressive." He calmly resumed his seat.

Puzzled, Renee asked, "Ummm, why didn't you eat me just now?"

She asked the question far too easily, and Archangelo fell silent.

A hush filled the compartment. Only the sounds of the train shivered the air between them. Just as the conversation seemed as if it might never begin again, the train clattered and swayed, and as if that had been a signal, Archangelo spoke. "…Did you want to die?"

His expression was cold, but Renee answered in her usual mild way. "Mm… No, I didn't. Besides, I can't stand pain."

"Then when you realized I was about to kill you, why didn't you react? At all?"

It was a perfectly natural question. Renee put a hand to her chin, thinking. Her words came out slowly, as if she was figuring out what to say as she said it. "Ummm… Well, to me, dying and being eaten by another immortal aren't quite the same thing."

"They aren't?"

"I think the meaning of an individual's life is in their accumulated memories, not in their will. That's not my opinion as a scientist, and it's heresy for an alchemist, but... Ummm, how do I put it...? Essentially, even if you'd eaten me, the way I see it, I wouldn't be dead. I'm not talking about souls or anything like that; I *am* the sum of my memories." Renee spoke haltingly but clearly. "When you wake up after a particularly sound sleep, don't you sometimes wonder whether you're the same person who fell asleep? I think you could say you are and also that you're not. The me who wanted cake yesterday may be a different person from the me who wants salad now. Your cells are constantly replacing themselves from one second to the next. The only part of you that stays the same is the information in the memories you've collected."

"What are you driving at?"

"To me, *that's all it is.* Whether I'm eating someone or being eaten by them. Even if I mingled with your memories, I would be myself, plus that new experience. That means you would be yourself, Archangelo, and at the same time, you would be me, I guess, or, um... Oh dear, I can't really put it into words..."

"No, I understand the gist." Expressionless, Archangelo heaved an even greater sigh. When he spoke again, his tone held a variety of emotions. "You really are yourself, Renee. I'm relieved, but now I'm skeptical in another way. Careless mistakes and failures constantly dog your actions. I can understand why that would make matters worse. However, you never deliberately took part in evil."

"Evil?"

"Forgive me, but from what I've seen of your activities at Nebula, there is nothing else to call it," Archangelo said bluntly.

Renee, who'd been tilting her head all this time, cocked it in the other direction. Sounding a little troubled, she murmured, "Really? So according to current moral standards, the things I've been doing at Nebula are bad..."

"I think they would be considered bad even by the old standards."

"I see. Yes, you're right. If what I'm doing is bad, then the police and all sorts of other people may get in my way. I'll have to be careful. Really, Archangelo, thank you for telling me," she said with a smile.

"......" He watched her with narrowed eyes. Then, gazing out the window at the scenery, he quietly said, almost to himself, "Had you been compelled to do that research instead of participating voluntarily, I'd intended to get rid of Nebula, but it appears that isn't the case."

In saying that he'd "get rid of" one of the world's leading corporations, Archangelo had made a very bold statement, but Renee didn't take it as a bluff. She let it go in one ear and out the other.

Archangelo continued, "I've determined that Nebula is not my enemy, and that in itself is a stroke of good fortune. If anything else comes up, I'll call on you again. Thank you for your cooperation."

Concluding what would have sounded like a business deal to anyone outside the situation, Archangelo slowly got up from his chair. As he was leaving, he glanced back at the view streaming past the window and made another remark, almost as an afterthought. "I also have a message from Professor Dalton."

"Professor Dalton! My, that takes me back! How is he?"

Without answering Renee's question, the youth impassively delivered the message.

"He says…'Be a little greedy.'"

It wasn't clear whether Archangelo understood what the words meant; his face was still expressionless.

Renee stared at him blankly, blinking. Then she gave a faint smile. "I do want things, you know. At the moment, I'm really looking forward to seeing what sort of condition my two daughters are in."

When Renee said "daughters," a slight change came over Archangelo's expression, but she didn't notice it. Still standing in front of the door, he took a long look at Renee's face. "…I'm told Huey Laforet gouged out that right eye of yours."

His own eyes held a cold, determined emotion, and the name "Huey" was thick with hatred as it left his mouth—not that Renee noticed.

"Well, it made us even. Huey really is mean, though," she said.

Even though Archangelo had just admonished Renee for her misdeeds, he said something ominous. "If you feel he's dangerous, shall I get rid of him?"

"Huh? Why?"

"Oh… I merely thought that a student who defied his teacher deserved to be punished harshly." The man's tone was harder than it had ever been, and his expression returned to his usual blank one.

However, Renee chided him. "You mustn't do that, Archangelo. Huey is your student and Dalton's, too, you know. No matter what happens, you mustn't abandon a student. Naughty." She sounded as though she were scolding a child, and Archangelo's expression softened slightly.

With a deep bow, he left the compartment.

⟺

As he stepped out into the corridor, the moment he closed the door, Archangelo's face tensed again, and he murmured to himself, "Huey Laforet…"

The hatred in his voice was even clearer than it had been a moment ago.

Their former pupil at the library, their most brilliant student. An alchemist who'd become immortal like them. A man who had felt no love for Renee, the woman Archangelo should have protected whatsoever, when he had slept with her.

A man whom the woman had accepted in an equally loveless way, as a mere experiment.

I will take the measure of this. Who among the writhing mass of immortals is harmful to Renee? If possible, I hope our student Huey's name is on the list of those I must eliminate.

Once, Archangelo had resolved to protect Renee, no matter what. To that end, he'd put distance between her and himself as well.

As a result, the fact that she'd gotten pregnant with her daughter had been a shock.

Even though he understood it had been nothing more than an "experiment" to her, he hadn't been able to come to terms with it.

If... If I had left my hand on Renee's head a moment longer...I might have given in to my own greed. I might have developed the illusion that doing so would let me have her to myself for eternity and thought, I want to eat.

Huey, I'm impressed you managed to control yourself.

His resolution to protect Renee hadn't lost its edge.

However, his personal jealousy toward Huey hadn't vanished, either, and as he walked down the train's corridor, complicated feelings churned inside him...

...along with deep regret over the fact that he himself hadn't managed to make a move.

⇐⇒

After she'd watched her alchemist acquaintance go, Renee began humming again. She took a fabric-wrapped object out of her bag.

When she unwound the cloth, a glass jar emerged. It contained a clear liquid, and a human eyeball had pressed itself against the side, writhing like a jellyfish.

"La-dum-doo-doo-doo-da-duuum. ♪ New York really is this way, isn't it?"

As she observed the eyeball's movements in the jar, she let her imagination travel in that direction.

"I'll be able to collect data on the people at Mist Wall, too. It's two birds with one stone!"

She talked about data collection in the exact same way she'd spoken of meeting her daughters.

The alchemist who couldn't discern a sense of obligation from desire gazed at the wriggling eyeball and kept on humming, wearing a little smile.

She didn't even notice the smile meant nothing at all.

Chapter 9   The Hitman Doesn't Hesitate

Claire Stanfield had been dead for several years.

At the end of 1931, while working as a conductor on the Flying Pussyfoot, a transcontinental express, he and a coworker had been killed by a terrorist in a shockingly cruel way: They'd had their faces ground off (although the specific method wasn't clear).

That was what the police records said at least.

His corpse had actually belonged to somebody else. Claire had taken over a name from a hitwoman he'd just happened to get acquainted with. He was alive and well as "Felix Walken."

The "Felix" name had originally belonged to a certain hired killer. When that man had retired, he'd handed over all traces of himself—his name and residence, as well as his fame and notoriety—to someone else. These things had passed through the hands of several professional killers in the space of a dozen years.

However, none of this really interested Claire, the current Felix.

Originally, he'd had an established rep as a hitman named Vino. As far as he was concerned, he'd lucked into a fresh start and a new place to belong. He didn't give it much thought beyond that.

That said, he was planning to keep the name "Felix" from getting around too much. Only a few people knew Claire was Vino, who would continue his life in the underworld as a mystery hitman.

That was how it was *supposed* to be.

"You're Felix Walken, aren't you?"

When a complete stranger flagged him down on the street, Felix—Claire—looked a little fed up as he turned around. He'd stressed his name change to Firo and his other friends tons of times, telling them, "The name's Felix, not Claire," but of course he didn't go around loudly introducing himself to people he didn't know.

It was the beginning of 1935. Half a day before the uproar at Firo's casino.

It had been only a few years since he'd changed his name, and he'd done practically nothing to make himself stand out. At this point in time, anyone who saw his face and called him Felix was probably bringing him trouble.

Pain in the ass, Claire thought, but as his eyes found the guy who'd spoken, he didn't show the slightest trace of fear. The guy was a total stranger.

Or rather, the *guys* were total strangers.

The group wore dark suits, and they were ostentatiously brawny. Their bulging muscles stretched their suits enough to create outlines in the fabric, and every one of them looked as if they'd been designed specifically to be intimidating.

"You've got the wrong guy. See ya." Giving them a casual wave, Claire walked away indifferently.

One of the toughs grabbed his shoulder firmly. "You've gotta know that ain't gonna throw us off, pal," the guy said with a snort.

Claire glanced back. "It looks like you know me pretty well..." Knocking away the big man's hand, he slowly turned to face the group. "In that case, you know I'm not somebody you can strong-arm or threaten, right?"

He hadn't made his voice particularly intimidating, but as far as he was concerned, the words were a warning. He'd decided that, if these guys really did know him, then they'd know that trying to force him was pointless.

If they change their tune and ask politely, maybe I should at least hear them out, Claire thought. However, the men chose a simpler route.

"You're still coming with us," said the man who'd grabbed his shoulder. There was a dangerous edge to his words.

"Gotta say, you fellas ain't exactly my idea of a good time. Where am I supposed to be going?"

"You don't need to know."

The men's attention was focused on Claire, their surroundings, and several cars that were stopped by the curbs. They were planning to muscle him into a car by force.

"Just so's you know, resisting is pointless," one of them said.

"Doesn't life get boring if everything you do has a point?" Claire gave a little sigh, then smiled at the big guy.

At the same time, he knocked the thug's thick ankles out from under him.

It had been a light sweep, and it shouldn't really have had the power to move anything. However, Claire's left hand had been on the man's shoulder, and he'd simultaneously applied pressure there. Thanks to the multiple forces at work, the big man's center of gravity had shifted, and he flipped, pivoting around a point near his waist.

In the next moment, while the man was airborne and horizontal, Claire set his right foot against the side of the thug's head—and stomped down.

"Bwuh...gah..."

The guy's spin accelerated rapidly, and his head slammed into the pavement. After a brief spasm, he was unconscious.

Without so much as glancing at him, Claire turned to the remaining men. "Sorry. It looks like he didn't understand, so I'll say it again: Force and threats won't work on me. Understand?" Nodding in response to his own comment, Claire added, "Well, I did strike first, so I'll cut you some slack and spare your lives. But listen, if I were you, I'd head home before I got hurt."

"...!"

In the span of a second, the brawny men had learned a lesson.

They'd heard that this man did anything, including murder, but the way he'd just moved... The leg he'd used to scoop his opponent's feet out from under him hadn't touched the ground before he'd raised it again, then stomped the man's head in midair. It really hadn't seemed like a maneuver an ordinary person could pull off.

They all gulped, and their thoughts went to the objects in their jackets.

The moment they started to wonder whether they should draw their heaters, their target—Handyman Felix—saw it coming and headed them off. "Uh, just FYI, if you're gonna use guns, I won't be able to go easy on ya. I mean, I *could*, but is it really worth the effort?"

When the men heard that, their hands all froze partway into their jackets.

Felix had been wearing an easygoing smile, but they'd picked up on the deadly intent beneath. His words were dripping with it.

The men had begun to sweat. The Handyman glanced at their faces, shrugged lightly, then looked at the cars. Noticing there were multiple shapes behind the windows, Felix crooked his index finger at them, calling the occupants over.

"Heeey, c'mon out. You don't want your precious underlings to bite the big one here, do you?"

A few seconds after Claire's taunt, there was movement in the row of cars.

The rear door of one car opened, and a lone man in aviator goggles stepped out. His hair was generously streaked with gray, but his face didn't seem that old. No sooner was he out of the car than he gave a brief gesture, ordering the goons to stand down.

As the big men beat a hasty retreat to one side of the road, Claire picked up on something odd.

There's nobody around.

He'd been walking down a lightly trafficked street a fair distance from central Manhattan, but still, there were almost no average Joes in sight.

Any normal person would have found this unsettling, but Claire didn't bat an eye.

I see. So I'm dealing with a bunch who can clear the street, although probably not the buildings.

Did that mean they were feds or members of one of the big mafia outfits? As he weighed various possibilities, Claire called to the white-haired man. "Hey there. Are you the boss of these fellas?"

The white-haired man threw back his slumped shoulders, straightening up. His spine cracked audibly. "Me, the boss? Perish the thought. I'm just a middle manager, Mr. Felix Walken."

"You've got the wrong guy. We've never met, have we? How would you know my name?"

"I heard it from someone who knows you."

"I see. Makes sense. Sorry for lying, sir. I'm Felix Walken. Your boys got a little too cheeky for me, so I knocked one of them down."

Claire (or Felix) suddenly adopted a much politer attitude, apologizing with startling ease.

The white-haired man wasn't sure how to respond to this. He hesitated for a moment, then cleared his throat. "Hmm. It's hard to say whether you're a liar or an honest man. Either way, it's a privilege to meet you, Handyman Felix."

Claire flashed a dauntless smile at the man. "No, the pleasure's all mine, Mr. Bartolo Runorata, supreme leader of the Runorata Family."

"……"

"…… " "…… " "……"

At Claire's words, the white-haired man and the big men who stood behind him silently exchanged looks. There was a chill in the air.

After the space of a few breaths, the manager responded, sounding troubled. "No… I'm not Mr. Runorata…"

"…"

"…Hello?"

"Nah, sorry about that. I was just irritated that people kept guessing my name right, so I said something random. Oh, guess that means I don't actually have to be polite? So, who're you, pal?" Claire returned to talking casually.

The white-haired man was taken aback, but only for a moment. Composing his face into an expressionless mask, he introduced himself.

"I'm Salomé... Salomé Carpenter."

"Sorry, not familiar. You seem like you're older than me. Should I be respecting my elders, at least?"

"No need. I don't intend to be polite with you, either." On the contrary, the man's voice held a faint trace of hostility. He examined Claire over from head to toe. "...You don't deviate from human standards; that's quite obvious. Did you really beat Christopher Shaldred?"

"Christopher?" At first, Claire wondered what the guy was talking about, but that name sounded familiar. After a moment, he smacked his hands together in realization. "Oh! Yeah, right! That guy! The red-eyed fella with the fangs!"

"...Precisely. I heard you'd defeated him at the Mist Wall building, when he was fighting in earnest."

"That's about the size of it! So what about him?"

Claire's answer had been excessively hearty. Salomé smiled thinly and ground his clenched teeth. "Well, he is *our creation*... A top-tier influential member of Lamia. It's quite hard to simply believe he was defeated."

"You should trust people, you know. Fellas who don't end up like this guy." Claire looked at the unconscious goon at his feet.

"No, no, I only believe what I've personally observed." Even as Salomé spoke, the big men backed up farther, beginning to disappear from the edge of Claire's vision.

"......?"

Claire almost asked what was going on, but he shoved the question back down. He'd already figured out the answer on his own.

Seven... No, eight of them?

He could sense there were more people around him now.

It wasn't that he had superpowers. He'd made the call based on the faint footsteps his ears had picked up.

That said, considering the fact that he'd managed to pick out faint noises made by people more than five yards away, any ordinary person might have thought it counted as a superpower.

Slowly turning around, he scanned his surroundings. There really were about eight new figures on the once-deserted street.

"What's with you fellas? You're a lot more colorful than that group of generic mooks back there."

The men and women Claire had spotted looked a bit different from ordinary civilians. They weren't exactly grotesque, but to a degree that put the earlier men in black suits to shame, they clearly weren't upright citizens.

They were a motley group. There was a man in a swallowtail coat who might have been headed to a dance; another who was naked to the waist; a young woman in an elegant gown with beautiful tattoos on her face and arms; a girl who was all bundled up, with a stocking cap pulled down so low it covered her eyes; and an individual in a skull mask who could have been any gender.

Even surrounded by this bizarre crew, Claire wasn't anxious, and he didn't scoff at their odd looks.

Instead, he reminisced.

They sorta remind me of the circus crowd. After all, it was more a collection of oddballs like these guys than a regular circus. I wonder how they're all doing.

As Claire basked in nostalgia, Salomé spread his arms and spoke slowly. "Like Christopher, they are members of Lamia. I hear they have a few thoughts regarding your defeat of their comrade."

"Huh. Yeah, they seem like a crew who would."

"Do you have anything to say to them?"

Salomé's expression betrayed no anxiety. He seemed to believe he had an absolute advantage.

Claire could tell these weren't just people in funny clothes. They were probably all at the top of their fields, whatever those happened to be. Even there, they were very similar to his companions from his circus days.

He felt a little kinship with them, and he gave them a smile. "Uh... Who was it again, your comrade Christopher? Yeah, I thrashed him." He scratched his cheek, a little bashful. "It's kinda embarrassing, but if you want to compliment me, I'll gladly accept it."

"......?" "?" "?"

The eccentrics seemed bewildered. Spreading his arms wide, Claire spoke in an extremely friendly way—with zero intent to taunt them.

"All right, go on. *Praise me* to your hearts' content."

⇔

On top of an old apartment building

On the roof of a six-story building, a figure was watching the Handyman, the researcher, and the members of Lamia, who'd frozen while their quarry talked. "So he's the one who defeated Christopher?"

"It looks like it."

"From what Leeza and Sham told me, I thought he'd be more of a monster. He looks surprisingly normal."

Grinning and enjoying himself, a man with black hair and golden eyes looked down at the redheaded Handyman. He was neatly dressed, but he had a bandage over one eye, which made for an odd combination. His name was Huey Laforet.

Beside him stood another man with a bandanna tied over his head. "He's the type who proves you can't judge a book by its cover," he said. "I bet that traumatized Leeza, too. He calls himself Felix Walken, but it's probably a pseudonym—"

"Claire Stanfield."

"...What?"

Huey had murmured the name out of nowhere. Tim, the captain of Huey's hand-trained unit Larva, frowned slightly.

"That is the young red-haired fellow's real name. According to official records, though, he's already dead, so it might be better to call him Felix," Huey said.

"……" *Crafty bastard. He knows more about this than I do.* Keeping his grievances bottled up, Tim sighed instead of objecting. Then he stared at the members of Lamia below. "…I see some unfamiliar faces."

"Yes, some of them haven't been added to Larva yet. I'll introduce them to you someday…as your new subordinates."

"As bosses go, I'm a figurehead. I bet I don't have the right to refuse." This time, Tim didn't bother to keep the sarcasm out of his voice.

"That's not true. If you'd rather not have them, they'll simply be fired. Granted, the thought of turning them out in this recession does pain me a bit…," Huey replied, without an ounce of pain in his voice.

Tim was about to feel even more irritated with him, but he pushed that away. He thought, *Well, maybe I should just be glad he didn't say, "We'll simply dispose of them."* Deciding there was no point in letting his personal grudge get any bigger, he slowly got his anger under control. "So what are you going to do with the Handyman?"

"That's a good question. What will happen to him?"

"Are you screwing with me?"

"Not at all. He isn't my subordinate. It would be presumptuous of me to do anything about him. I can put pressure on him, but what will he do in response…? In a way, my goal is the very act of observing the results. Although, that's true of most things, not just him." Giving a faint smile, Huey went on with lukewarm enthusiasm. "I really would have preferred for Adele, Frank, Chi, and the rest to be there as well. However, it would be problematic for you if he ended up taking them all out of commission, wouldn't it?"

So he didn't mind if everyone who was down there now did get taken out of commission. It didn't seem like a great thing for an employer to say. Tim frowned. "Look… What is it you want to do?" It was a rather unusual way of speaking to a superior.

Huey didn't seem bothered. He responded casually. "I just want to know all sorts of things." Then he quietly added, "Like that twisted 'demon'."

"...Demon?"

"It's nothing. My driving principle is the thirst for knowledge, nothing more." Huey smiled, and Tim shook his head slightly.

"No. There's something beyond that for you."

"Oh?"

"You've got some other, clearer goal, and that's why you're trying to learn everything. That's what it feels like anyway."

"I rather like that keen mind of yours."

Huey shrugged, complimenting his subordinate, and shamelessly evaded his question.

"Well, it's a personal matter, so we'll say it's a secret."

He was like a boy hiding the fact that he had a girlfriend.

Ordinarily, Huey wore a smile with no feeling behind it, but there almost seemed to be some sort of emotion in this one.

That smile convinced Tim it would be pointless to ask anything else. Wordlessly, he looked back at the scene below them.

Just then, with impeccable timing, things began to move.

⇔

The alley

A minute or so before Tim looked at the group in the alley from the roof...

"...That's a shocker. Who'd have thought you'd resort to cheap provocation at a time like this." Salomé shrugged as he spoke. Meanwhile, although the bizarre Lamia members had been standing there stunned, anger began to show in their expressions.

Claire scanned the group, cocking his head as if he was mystified. "This isn't what I was told," he commented briefly.

"...What isn't, Mr. Handyman Felix?"

"Well, when that Christopher fella came and picked a fight with me, I asked him what was in it for me if I took him up on that fight? What would I get out of beating him?" Claire sounded annoyed at the others' anger toward him as he forged ahead. "And he told me, 'If you beat me, you can brag about it to the rest of Lamia.' So I figured I could do a little bragging and get some compliments, y'know? After all, he said I'd get something out of this. If you just get mad about it, I'm not getting anything good unless I'm a masochist. Right?"

" " " " " " " " " " " " " " " "

The other nine people present all went silent at once.

Most of them were looking at Claire, wondering, *Is this guy an idiot?*

Speaking for the group, Salomé candidly divulged his own feelings. "Christopher is a problem as well, but...is that the reason you engaged him in mortal combat?"

"Hmm? Oh, he came to kill me, but I didn't need to kill him, so you can't really call it 'mortal combat,'" Claire answered. "Ah, sorry, that was nitpicky. Frankly, yeah, I did fight him for a reason like that, and I won, so I don't appreciate getting bawled out."

At that, one of the members of Lamia—the woman with the tattooed face—broke her silence. "You went a round with Chris so people you'd never even met would compliment you? Are you nuts?"

Pivoting toward her, Claire spread his arms and made a declaration to the whole group. "Of course! I love getting compliments! Even if they're insincere or downright lies! That means killing me with compliments actually works. Besides, if that Christopher guy is such a special comrade to you, shouldn't you at least compliment me superficially, so you don't make him a liar?" Claire kept talking nonstop, like a professional storyteller. Then, suddenly, he seemed to remember something; he pointed an index finger skyward and gave them a caveat.

"Oh, but I hate being called a genius, so watch that one. I've got the abilities I have now through hard work, not talent. *Genius* doesn't sound good; it makes you picture some lazy bum who's tough without putting in any effort. That's bad, see?"

He rattled off, assuming compliments were a foregone conclusion. The members of Lamia had no idea what to do. His words alone seemed to have dragged them into his orbit. Looking at them, Salomé sighed deeply. "Enough. Let's begin the experiment. Don't kill him, though. Our job is to bring him in, nothing more."

Salomé was acting as if there was no room for argument, and Claire shrugged. "Just ask me politely. Nobody has to get hurt that way. And by 'nobody,' I mean you."

"That wouldn't be much of an experiment. Besides, you may all end up working under the same person after this. It would be good to see who ranks higher, wouldn't it?"

As Salomé finished speaking, the surrounding mood changed. Claire had befuddled Lamia, but they seemed to have remembered their job—and that he was their enemy.

"You're kind of a jerk-off. Hey, fellas, working for somebody like him must be rough. You've got my sympathies," Claire said. "That being the case, lemme ask: Are you really okay with this?"

"?"

"I know that guy wants to see what I've got, but you don't stand a chance. If I beat you here, you'll just be losers. You could do the unexpected and side with me instead. What do you say?"

The Handyman had openly invited them to secede, right in front of their boss.

The proposal seemed to have come out of left field for the group. A few of them looked bewildered—but the rest clearly hated him now.

"Beating Christopher seems to have given you a swelled head," the tattooed woman told him.

"You think? Nah, I was like this before I flattened him."

"...You're selling us pretty short. You don't think one of us might be stronger than you?"

"Hmm, could be. I'm really strong, and I'm confident I won't lose to anybody. And of course I gotta be stronger than everybody for my baby Chané, but... Well, I won't deny the possibility itself."

Claire seemed to be looking back over his own life.

"But let's say, hypothetically, that one of you was stronger than me."

He surveyed the men and women around him, and there was a hint of contempt in his eyes as he continued speaking.

"You'd gang up on a guy who was weaker than you, eight to one? ...Isn't that embarrassing?"

⇔

On the roof

"...Why are they all just standing there?"

Watching the people below, Tim tilted his head, perplexed. He'd figured they'd have a brawl on their hands in no time, but for some reason, nobody was moving.

He'd thought Salomé might have been giving one of the long speeches he was known for, but even so, this was weird. Tim's face, which had been sullen to begin with, grew even sterner.

From beside him, Huey said, "This is intriguing. It seems he's more than a wild animal."

"Not necessarily. He might be begging for his life."

"That would be its own kind of intriguing, so I wouldn't take issue with it." Huey sounded aloof.

Tim raised an eyebrow, getting ready to complain—but then he decided that whatever he said would have no effect, so he just returned his attention to the alley.

⇔

The alley

"Hey, Salomé. Can we kill this guy? We can kill him, right?" asked the tattooed woman.

The murderous hostility in her voice was clear, but the Handyman responded before Salomé could.

"Well, simmer down. There's another reason I want to avoid doing this eight-on-one." Claire folded his arms, nodding away with arbitrary conviction. "If we go through with this, I'm going to demolish you. In simple terms, I'll work you over. If you lost to me all on my own, you'd lose face."

"......?"

The others looked as if they were wondering, *What the hell is this guy talking about?*, but the Handyman kept going. "So let's do this instead! We'll count the guy with goggles over there and split our group into two teams for a five-on-five match! That way, whichever team wins, we can say it was on the level, that we fought fair and square! Woohoo!"

The Handyman grinned with satisfaction. He seemed to think he'd hit on a terrific idea, and at that, the people around him finally caught on.

This man hadn't been saying and doing weird things to provoke them. He was genuinely just speaking his mind.

It was as if he was *describing a fate that would inevitably come to pass* in order to make the situation more fun for himself.

This was no mere world ruler. He spoke with the arrogance of an absolute god, one who determined his own destiny. Although his proposal sounded utterly daft, if he actually had the skills to back it up, its significance would change drastically.

At the very least, this wasn't a cheap trick to unsettle them. While it would have been great if he were a garden-variety delusional idiot, they'd already heard that he'd defeated Christopher, so they knew he wasn't pulling their leg.

Someone had been selling somebody short, but it wasn't the Handyman. It was them.

Up until that very moment, they'd thought Christopher's loss had been some sort of fluke or that one of his peculiar whims had made him do it. However, they were the ones who hadn't been thinking. They hadn't considered the possibility that this man might actually be a formidable foe.

Trained soldiers might not have been so careless.

However, Lamia—and particularly the members who were there—had never fought anyone with greater physical abilities and combat skills than theirs. Chi and Sickle had experienced defeat, and if either of them had been there, things might have been different.

"It's too bad Chi and Sickle aren't here. I bet Chi would say, 'That's all that matters,' and wrap this up." The tattooed woman tsked in irritation. She and the rest of the group were no longer angry at Claire. Instead, a sharper hostility filled the alley.

They had an accurate handle on the situation now. The man in front of them was a kind of enemy they'd never faced before.

The savage atmosphere grew thicker and more viscous, coiling around Claire from head to toe. When he spoke to Lamia, he was wearing a smile that was different from the type he'd worn a moment ago. "Okay, then. You, you, you over there...and you. You're on my team."

He was genuinely planning to split the group into teams. He picked four individuals at random: the man in the swallowtail coat; the character in the skull mask; the bundled-up girl with the stocking cap; and the tattooed woman in the formal gown, the one who'd shown him the most hostility.

However, the Lamia members were no longer bewildered by what he said. They simply waited for their orders. Salomé, whose face was perfectly expressionless, raised a hand.

He'd probably realized it wouldn't be possible to keep his subordinates from fighting to kill at this point.

Erasing his emotions as much as possible and preparing to observe every moment of the scene that was about to play out, Salomé called:

"Let the experiment begin."

He murmured the words in a detached way. No sooner had he finished than several members of Lamia launched themselves into action. Fire exploded in the alley they'd cleared of people.

*   *   *

Claire slowly spread his arms.

In the storm of hate-filled determination—he spoke as if even their drive to kill him was precious to him.

"Welcome to my world."

He was wearing a ferocious smile that made anyone who saw it feel a bottomless chill.

"...Bring it on, extras."

⟺

On the roof

"There they go. Finally." With his eyes on the group, Tim exhaled wearily. "Let's just hope nobody dies."

"You think Lamia is at a disadvantage, Tim?"

"No clue. I mean, I don't even know those guys."

"You aren't going to let that go, are you? Take this opportunity to learn about them, if you would." Lightly deflecting the sarcasm, Huey also focused on the melee that was unfolding below.

And then he picked up on something—it was indeed a *melee*.

"Oho." He chuckled.

"Huh...? What's up?"

A few seconds after Huey, Tim noticed it as well. According to the plan, the eight Lamia members—everyone but Salomé—were supposed to pin down Felix. Instead, the situation seemed to have gotten rather complicated. "Infighting...? No, that's not it..." What was happening didn't make sense.

After all, while the Handyman was definitely fighting members of Lamia, for some reason, he was fighting only four of them.

Being up on the roof with a bird's-eye view of the situation was what let Tim understand how strange it was.

All eight members were attacking the Handyman as a group.

However, while the Handyman turned aside all their ferocious attacks, he was striking back against only four specific opponents.

Salomé was standing a little distance away. If they included him in the count, it looked as though two teams of five had begun by fighting each other, and then one team had fractured and was now attacking one of its members from behind—

That was what had made Tim assume it was infighting. The Handyman and Lamia had never been a team, though, so that word couldn't possibly apply.

Huey was gazing at the alley, looking rather entertained. Tim ignored him, and as he realized just how eerie the Handyman was, his eyebrows drew together.

"What the hell is going on down there?"

⟺

In the alley

Although the situation was confusing to Tim, to anyone who'd been listening in on their conversation, it was quite simple.

Claire had arbitrarily designated four Lamia members as "teammates."

Of course, those four were also trying to attack him, but he evaded skillfully, striking back at the four he'd designated "enemies."

Naturally, the members of Lamia weren't just punching and kicking. There was one who fought with a foreign martial art that was almost unknown in America at that time, and another who used his abnormally long legs as if they were hands, and yet another who used their inhumanly good kinetic vision to read Claire's movements, then they flung multiple throwing knives at the places where those movements seemed likely to take him.

However, Claire's motions and judgment calls surpassed all of them. They were beyond the pale of common sense.

Although the blades flew at him as if they could tell where he was going, he not only evaded them but sometimes caught them and hurled them at different opponents.

On top of that, in situations where the Lamia members he'd designated as allies would be hit if he evaded, he protected them by knocking the projectiles out of the air instead.

Not only did he avoid attacking the people he'd arbitrarily claimed as teammates, he was diligently protecting them.

While his behavior was shredding Lamia's pride, the members couldn't even afford to care.

Am I really fighting one *guy?* Cold sweat broke out on the tattooed woman's back.

She'd been fighting for less than a minute, but she'd already built up an extraordinary amount of fatigue. It felt like taking on a whole band of powerful martial artists at once.

The mental pressure did more to shake her desire to fight than her physical fatigue did. She even briefly considered the delusional idea that they were facing a ferocious animal shapeshifter.

Dammit. If Miz Sickle were here... After that thought passed, she felt a pang of shame for thinking of an absent companion during a fight.

The tattooed woman twisted her torso. Making full use of her extraordinarily elastic muscles and flexible joints, she turned more than 180 degrees, and then, blade in hand, she unwound herself, using her momentum to slash at the Handyman's back with the speed of a whip.

However, he dodged by a hair and vanished.

"!"

Where is he?!

She and the other members of Lamia darted their attention from one way to the next, trying to find their opponent. In time, their eyes fell on the Handyman as he stood behind the girl with the stocking cap, whom he'd picked as a teammate, with his hands on her shoulders. He must have been pressing some sort of muscular or nervous pressure point; he was holding the girl's shoulders lightly, but her arms just hung there, trembling. She didn't seem to be able to raise them.

The Handyman smiled gently. *"Poison's not allowed."*

"?!"

"If you diffuse it from there, you'll take out your teammates."

"...!"

The girl with the stocking cap hid her eyes, but everybody could tell she was aghast.

She wasn't the only one. The members of Lamia knew about her unique ability, and they were just as shocked.

Her special technique involved scattering a variety of poisons that she'd hidden under her thick clothing.

However, the only ones who knew this were her comrades in Lamia and Rhythm, the research team Salomé led. Huey Laforet probably knew about it from reports he'd been given, but there was no possible way this guy should have known about it, especially since she hadn't made any actual moves yet.

"How...did you know?" The girl's voice was so faint it was practically inaudible, but Claire responded.

"Huh? Well, with your build, it didn't seem like you'd be using martial arts or a big clunky gun, so I figured it was either bombs or poison. Then I saw you were trying to stay upwind from me all the time, so I figured it had to be poison."

Salomé had been observing from a distance, and when he overheard, the look in his eyes changed. In less than a minute of mayhem, the man had spared attention for such subtleties. Not only that, but he'd also shut her down just as she was about to use it. Salomé was now sure this man was completely different from any specimen he'd ever encountered.

A perfect human.

That cheap phrase crossed the researcher's mind, but he immediately rejected the idea as a misguided delusion.

Still, he had to admit the fellow was extraordinary.

Christopher is my masterpiece, and in terms of basic physical abilities and reflexes, the people here aren't his inferiors.

And yet… Am I to believe a human is fighting eight of them at once, under a special self-inflicted handicap no less, and he's still surpassing them? That's ludicrous. He'll destroy the definition of human.

The other Lamia members had stopped moving as soon as the Handyman had pinned the girl in the stocking cap. They hadn't been trained as cold-blooded assassins, which meant they didn't have it in them to abandon a companion for the sake of defeating an enemy. On the contrary, the guinea pigs of Lamia were more conscious of being part of a team than most humans, and even attempting to teach them to fight like that might have been pointless.

Repressing the various thoughts that ran through his mind, Salomé gave the man an indifferent and rather ironic compliment. "Good lord. I never dreamed you'd be such a troublesome test subject. One would think you were a genuine vampire."

Claire smiled, making small talk in the middle of such deep hostility coming at him from all angles. "There was a guy in my circus who called himself a vampire, but he looked normal compared to the lot of you. The most he did was wear a suit and a sparkly hat."

Salomé smiled thinly. "I know nothing about the sartorial preferences of vampires. Now then…you and I are on opposing teams, correct?" Turning that faint smile toward the ground, Salomé slowly spread his arms. "If I don't join the game soon, they'll accuse me of negligence."

Then, looking around at the members of Lamia, he shook his head regretfully. "Still… I failed badly in my selection of test equipment. It looks as though I should reset the experiment."

⟺

On the roof

"This is going nowhere… And hey, whoa, Salomé—!" Tim had been watching Salomé's movements from the roof, and there was real anxiety in his voice.

That maniac researcher—is he going to do that?!

What does he think we cleared people out of here for anyway?! The hell's wrong with him?!

Tim knew what the man was about to do, and he knew what the results would be.

Is that bastard planning to break the Lamias along with the target?! What if the Handyman is the only one who survives, huh?! What then?!

No, it's even worse than that—if we stay here, he'll get us, too!

He screamed the words silently, but he had a feeling shouting at Salomé would do nothing. He said out loud, "Not good! If he pulls *that*, the Bureau of Investigation is definitely going to catch on..." He had to tell Huey they needed to make tracks—for now, at least. He whipped around—

—but no one was there. Only the bleak roof spread out in front of him.

"Huh?"

Huey—did he take off without me?!

Tim's cheeks tensed. Hastily, he looked left, right, up, and down, then promptly realized his error.

Out of the corner of his eye, for one brief moment, he glimpsed a figure. As he turned to look—he saw that figure drop into the space between the building and its neighbor.

"Hu— Huey?!"

Flustered, he leaned out and saw Huey casually plummeting from the roof as lightly as a drifting feather. As he fell, he kicked window frames and projections in the walls, skillfully breaking his momentum.

He wasn't falling. He was descending by the fastest available method. Understanding this, Tim turned his gaze to heaven and clutched his head.

What happened to watching how this played out?!

He spat his next complaint through gritted teeth:

"Besides, what's the point of having you on the front line?!"

⟺

A few seconds earlier   In the alley

"—?!"

When they saw what Salomé was doing, the members of Lamia tensed.

Claire was still holding the shoulders of the girl in the stocking cap, and he felt her start to tremble with fear.

He's up to something, huh. Claire narrowed his eyes.

The tattooed woman shouted, "Hold it, Salomé! What are you doing?!"

Behind Salomé's goggles, his teary eyes were filled with remorse. "It's all right. I love all of you... Yes, I do love you! So don't worry!"

This is bad. I bet he's going to pull something nastier than poison, Claire thought.

Naturally, the idea that Claire might die here didn't even occur to him. However, he decided it was going to be tough to completely protect the four members of Lamia he'd designated as allies. They might have been enemies to begin with, but Claire thought that not following rules he'd set for himself was a shameful thing, and he tried to come up with a way to save them.

In less than a second, he'd made up his mind.

I guess I'll crush him before he does anything.

Claire moved fast. Releasing the girl's shoulders, he tugged on her arm lightly.

She was holding a little bottle of the poison she'd been planning to use.

"Oh..."

The girl made a small noise, and Claire apologized in a whisper. *("If this stuff is lethal, I'm sorry.")*

He wasn't planning to use it on her, but he might end up killing her boss.

Apologizing for that in advance, Claire swiped the bottle out of the girl's hand. Fear had loosened her grip, and he didn't give her a chance to argue. The bottle held a powder; she'd probably been planning to seed the wind with it. He tensed, preparing to lob the container directly at Salomé's face—but at the last second, his peerless kinetic vision and reflexes aborted the throw.

He'd realized that Salomé had frozen and that he was watching a point above Claire's shoulder—in other words, something behind and slightly above Claire—with a shocked expression on his face.

Claire didn't know specifically what the man had been attempting to do, but something had obviously happened.

With the little bottle still in his hand, Claire whipped around and saw a slim man. He'd appeared in the alley abruptly and was wearing a mechanical smile.

"Wha...?" "That's nuts..." "Why is he here?"

The members of Lamia had spotted the man soon after Claire did, and they all sounded startled.

The slim man shot a casual glance at them, then spoke to the man who was farthest from him. "Salomé, you mustn't get violent."

His tone had been mild, but Salomé's eyes widened, and he made a hasty apology. "I...I'm terribly so— Terribly sorry!" His composure had vanished without a trace; his face was pale and shiny with sweat.

From Salomé's attitude, Claire realized the newcomer must have been the mastermind behind this incident. However, before he pursued that issue, he asked about something that had been bothering him. "Fella... Did you come down here from up there?"

"Yes. Long ago, I wore a mask and played at being an acrobat. I'm used to it." For reasons unknown, this admission seemed to have some emotional significance for the man. Then he focused on Claire—and in a firm yet gentle tone, he apologized. "Speaking as their employer, please forgive my subordinates for their rudeness."

When they heard the apology from Huey Laforet, their boss, the tattooed woman and the other members of Lamia trembled.

As always, his voice had been almost pleasant. However, those who knew he was a terrorist and national public enemy couldn't help suspecting that, behind that smile, there was nothing but an endless void. One might have called it a cool pressure. The kinder Huey's voice, the colder the sweat that trickled down their spines.

The Handyman's instincts were preternaturally sharp. No doubt he'd gauged Huey's true nature in the blink of an eye.

Despite Master Huey's power, the tattooed woman was certain that even he couldn't tame this guy.

Handyman Felix was abnormal. He believed, deeply and sincerely, that the world was his. There was no way any threat would work on somebody like that.

This Felix guy might just manage to permanently kill Huey's indestructible body. As far as mankind was concerned, this guy was a singularity.

The ruler and the immortal—no matter who won, the ending would be costly.

Both were about to bet everything they had and try to take everything from their opponent.

She and the others were going to have to witness the results, no matter what they were.

Her group had been created as incomplete immortals, those who drifted aimlessly between these two concepts: human and inhuman. How should they live? This fight might show them.

Swallowing hard, the members of Lamia took a step back from Felix, deciding to watch the situation play out.

An unsettling wind blew through the spaces between the buildings.

Once the wind died down, Handyman Felix spoke. "Those eyes. Your face..."

"?" "?" "???"

Question marks rose in the minds of Salomé and the rest of the audience. They hadn't been expecting an opener like that at all.

"You wouldn't happen to be...Chané's big brother?"

That was the last name they expected to hear.

"Chané" was the name of Huey's daughter.

Because they knew this, the tattooed woman and the others grew even more confused.

Before his bewildered subordinates, Huey boldly pointed out the other man's mistake. "No, I'm her father. People do often assume I'm young, but...I'm simply immortal. My apologies."

The Handyman's reaction to that statement was dramatic. He stood up straighter and held out his right hand like a diplomat. "I'm Felix Walken. It's an honor to make your acquaintance, sir."

His former arrogance had vanished, and he took the hand of the man in front of him—his future father-in-law—as if he were just a regular guy. "Really, thank you, sir. Thank you so much for bringing Chané into my world!" He shook his hand firmly, effusively expressing his gratitude. He actually seemed a bit more worked up than an ordinary man would have been. "Your daughter is graciously allowing me to court her. Frankly, I don't think marriage is too far off."

"Well, well. She's far from perfect, but I hope you'll treat her well," Huey responded with a smile. Then, still wearing that smile, he broached another topic. "By the way, Handyman Felix. I would like to engage you for a job."

"Well, how about that. May I ask what it is?" In high spirits, Felix started talking business.

Huey looked around. "This isn't really the place for a discussion. Shall we find a different venue? You are my daughter's first beau. Do let me treat you to dinner."

"Gladly, sir!"

"Then... Is there room for the two of us in your car, Salomé?"

Finding himself abruptly addressed, Salomé came to himself with a jolt. He cleared his throat, adjusting the tail of his coat and the position of his goggles. Then, completely switching gears, he walked to the car with measured steps. Opening the rear door, he stood by courteously.

"All right. Let me convey you to your dinner engagement."

Salomé was acting like a butler, and they didn't keep him waiting. Huey and Felix started toward the car. They passed by the petrified Lamia members as if nothing had happened.

Pausing beside the girl with the stocking cap, Felix put the bottle of poison back in her hand, folding her fingers around it. "Thanks for the loan. Poison's dangerous, so be careful how you handle it, all right?"

"Huh…? Oh, yes…"

The girl's response seemed to satisfy Felix. Humming, he walked off with Huey.

"What was it about Chané that attracted you?"

"Everything."

"My goodness."

Continuing their amiable conversation, the two climbed into the car. Leaving almost everyone else behind, they nonchalantly faded from the scene.

"……"

"………"

"……………?"

"? ?! ??? ? ……?!"

The members of Lamia were stunned.

After Huey and Felix had gotten into the car, Salomé had taken the front passenger seat, and they'd pulled away without a single word for the crew they were abandoning at the scene. The Lamia stood there in silence.

The development had been far too much, and they weren't able to get the situation straight in their heads. For a little while, they couldn't move.

From beside them, a voice spoke.

"Hi there. I'm Tim. I manage Larva. Nice to meet you." He wore a bandanna tied around his head, and he pushed his glasses up. "As your new boss, I've got one brief note regarding the results of this maneuver."

The words he said next almost seemed to be directed at himself.

"Assume everything about that ginger was a nightmare and forget him. That is all."

Chapter 10   The Fugitive's Den Has No Blanket

Like any other nation, America had many faces.

Some of those facets were bright and glamorous, but of course the nation had poverty as well, and in the shadow of the unprecedented Great Depression, that negative aspect had undermined vast swaths of society.

The government was fighting back with the New Deal, but it would be a little longer before the economy recovered.

The Depression had begun several years ago.

Riots over food had broken out repeatedly all over the country, but those who were able to riot were still doing better than some. In certain states, there were reports that the unemployed had gone hungry for so long they didn't have the strength to protest anymore. Since more and more people were having trouble paying for their electricity, there were various districts that didn't have a single light on at night.

The wealthy were surrounded by bright light even during the recession, and they could use indoor heating to stave off the cold. However, while the poor might look for jobs, there were none to be had, and they couldn't extricate themselves from their circumstances.

During those dreary years, multiple workhouses went under, and the streets overflowed with drifters.

As the shadow of the Depression continued to constrict many lives, the government kept fighting it through a variety of measures, one of which was building more welfare lodging houses.

*　　　*　　　*

This particular lodging house had been thrown together rapidly and financed not by the government but by a certain doctor.

It was located on the outskirts of New York, and its atmosphere was completely different from Millionaires' Row, where the affluent lived. Those who had lost their homes huddled here, living quietly with their families.

The house had been set up by a doctor named Fred. He'd bought a shuttered hotel and was using it just as it was. He'd originally intended to reuse it as a hospital but had decided to convert it into a lodging house until the Depression ended, as a place where the unemployed could get off the streets and out of the cold.

He charged the lowest rent possible for rooms, but when expenses were taken into account, this was a charity project on which he was prepared to take a loss.

However, even with the Depression, the people who passed through this lodging house didn't have to worry about starving quite yet. Until just the other day, they'd had temporary work.

On the coast, very near to the island of Manhattan, was an avant-garde building that had been nicknamed Ra's Lance. It had been designed as a multipurpose commercial building, and many of the local residents had been roped in to help build it. The unveiling ceremony was already over, but parts of the basement were still under construction, and many people from this lodging house were working at the site. Some of them used the money they'd earned on the job to find better places to live, and so rooms sometimes opened up at the lodging house.

On one such day, a man practically dived into a vacant room.

The place was really too cramped to be considered a room. The only things in it were a bed and minimal furnishings. Spiders and rats ate each other in the corners, and angry roars, sobs, and the occasional scream echoed from all sides.

"...Well, I guess it's better than the welfare housing I saw earlier."

Lodging houses were housing in name only, where penniless prostitutes and down-and-out thugs gathered. Most of the rooms didn't have electricity. Relying on candles for light meant fires broke out frequently, and even though people often died, conditions were never improved.

Telling himself this was good compared to places like that, the man wearily lowered himself onto the edge of the bed.

Yeah, that's right. If I'm hearing yelling and screaming from my neighbors, it means they've still got the energy to make noise. Really, I'm the one who wants to howl, but I don't have it in me... Well, tons of people bunk down without a roof over their heads. Compared to them, I'm a lucky fella.

Now, if only I didn't have pursuers on my tail...

Nader Schasschule reviewed his position.

He'd been practically kidnapped by a guy named Ladd Russo and brought to New York. Come to think of it, at that point, it seemed as if some nasty current of events had swirled around his feet and trapped them.

If that Ladd fella hadn't glommed on to me, right about now, I'd be...

......

Where would I be now?

That's when it hit him: He'd already been out of options.

Nader hadn't wanted to leave prison in the first place. The Bureau of Investigation had talked him around, and he'd figured that the few remaining Lemures would have forgotten about a schmuck like him by now. At this point, he was well aware he'd been way too naïve.

And anyway, who were the fellas who were watching us after we got out?

There were mysterious people shadowing them, the trouble at the casino, and then—

Even that waitress. She looked like she coulda been anybody, and even she was part of that outfit. Part of Hilton...!

Outside the casino, he'd encountered a girl. A mixture of hate and murderous malice had suffused her young face as soon as she'd seen him.

It had been half a day since then, and he still couldn't get that sight out of his head.

*   *   *

From that point on, he'd run and kept on running. He'd slipped into a group of working stiffs who'd just gotten off the job and wound up at this lodging facility. When he asked the staff member who was doling out food, the guy had said a room had just opened up, and they'd been about to put out an ad for it.

Maybe the man had succumbed before Nader's sheer desperation, or maybe handing him several bills with the injunction to pad his wages with them had done the trick. Either way, he'd managed to become the tenant of this little room.

He bought a pillow from a nearby store, pulled all the cotton out of it, and stuffed it with the bundles of bills he'd gotten at the casino.

As Nader worked, he sighed wearily. *I'm like a bad joke. I duped the fellas above me over and over, fighting my way up...*

And now, even though I'm rolling in dough, I have to fake like I'm poor and dupe everybody here.

Nader Schasschule was a flimflam artist.

That said, he had only tried to talk a rich person into an investment scam once.

For him, it was more a way of life than an occupation. He'd trick the strong, convincing them he'd be useful, then crush the organization he'd just left. After that, when he'd sensed he couldn't move any further up the ranks of his new organization, he'd start to look outside the group, find a stronger outfit—and begin to sell himself to it with no hesitation whatsoever.

He'd sold people out like this over and over, worming his way into ever-stronger outfits, climbing the ladder.

However, he hadn't been able to use Huey Laforet's Lemures as a stepping-stone. As a matter of fact, he'd put his foot wrong and slipped right off the ladder. Miraculously, he'd survived. Even so, as things stood, they'd ruined him.

Why had things ended up like this? He mulled that over as he stuffed money into his pillow.

Why had he become a grifter? What had his first scam been?

He'd kept thinking about those things the whole time he'd been lying low in prison, fearing retaliation from Huey's underlings.

If it hadn't been for that beginning, none of this would have happened to him. He would have inherited his dad's cornfield, and although he didn't know whether he would have been happy, at least life would have been peaceful.

However, the more he thought about it, the more certain he was of the answer. As he sewed the end of the cut pillow closed again, the same answer came to mind, and he saw the familiar scenery of his good old hometown.

His very first scam had been a lie he'd told to a childhood friend, a girl who was quite a bit younger than he was.

When I grow up, I'm gonna be a hero!

Yeah, like Wyatt Earp or Jesse James!

Just you watch—I'll get super strong!

And then, hey... I could protect you, too, if you want.

Someone had bullied the girl, and she'd been crying. He'd told her that little white lie to comfort her. To set her mind at ease.

"Although...at the time, I didn't think I was lying," Nader muttered to himself, dropping the pillow full of money onto the bed. He'd really meant those words when he'd said them in the moment. He'd wanted to be a hero and protect her. That had been his dream.

However, in the end, he'd become a run-of-the-mill con artist. He hadn't even been able to swindle a fortune for himself. He was a former terrorist turned traitor, lying low in what was basically a workhouse.

As far as "heroes" went, people who were on the brink of starving to death with their integrity intact fit the definition better than him, a guy who'd just won a ton of money at a casino.

Even if he'd genuinely believed those words as a kid, if this was what he was like now, he'd flat out lied to her.

Oh, wow!

That's amazing! You're so keen, Nader!

If it's you, I'm sure you'll get really, really strong!

That's a promise, Nader!

Every time he remembered his childhood friend's innocent, delighted smile, guilt squeezed his heart again.

She'd smiled because she'd believed in him with all her heart.

But after ten years, his memories were hazy in places.

He had to recall her face more vividly.

In an attempt to ease his own fear a little, Nader tried to lose himself in memories of his hometown, but his young friend's face suddenly twisted with hatred, and she spat out a curse at him.

"Death to traitors."

Her twisted face looked exactly like that waitress's.

"DwaAAah?!"

Nader flinched, startled, and tumbled off the bed.

The pain when his back hit the floor brought him to his senses, and he realized he'd almost fallen asleep sitting up.

"A…a dream, huh…?"

He'd broken out in a full-body cold sweat, and his breathing was as rough as if he'd just run a sprint. The face of his childhood friend had temporarily vanished from his memory, overwritten by that waitress's face.

Dammit!

What is this? What's with them? They almost killed me… They killed everybody else who'd sold them out with me… And even then— even then they can't forgive me?!

"……"

Resuming his seat on the bed, he took close to a minute to get his breathing under control. Then his thoughts went to the woman, who had to be one of Huey's people…

…and also to the question of what he should do now.

Her encounter with Nader had seemed to be a genuine coincidence; he didn't think she'd been tailing him, but that was a problem in and of itself. After all, it meant Huey's people were so thick in this town that he'd run into one by accident. Of course, it was possible only a handful of Huey's underlings were here and this had been an unlucky coincidence… But either way, now that they'd spotted him, he was in just as much danger.

He'd considered making tracks off the island, but they might have lookouts posted on the bridges. Besides, if he took to his heels on his own again, it wouldn't change the slow downward spiral he was stuck in. Meaning he had to do some thinking, right this minute.

What would it take to save him?

What could he do to clear the books?

If he joined a group of tramps and working stiffs, the men who roved around the country looking for food and work, he might be able to cover his tracks to some extent. As a matter of fact, if it hadn't been for the money he'd accidentally picked up at the casino, he probably would have ended up in that life anyway, even if he hadn't been on the run.

However, due to some bizarre quirk of fate, he'd come into the sort of jackpot you got from hitting a triple seven. He wouldn't be hard up for food or shelter for a while. If he played his cards right, he might even manage to start up a business in the Depression.

…But a run-in with robbers would finish him.

He could have put the money in a bank. The thing was, depositing a big sum of money just after he'd been released might attract the wrong sort of attention from the Bureau of Investigation, and more than anything, Huey's information network might pick up on him.

Dammit… What is this? What the hell?! Why would they chase around a bottom-rung flunky like me for years and years? What do they get outta that?!

Anger rose inside him, but not enough to squash the fear.

"Dammit…"

For now, I'll get some rest. I'll think after that.

Being short on sleep wasn't helping his mind work any better. Thinking he might as well make the most of the bed he'd managed to find, Nader lay down.

"…No blanket, huh?"

In a cold month like this one, he thought he might freeze, but he didn't have the courage to go outside again to buy a blanket. Besides, he'd hidden his money in the pillow; if he was dumb enough to take his eyes off it, he might lose it to an oblivious pillow thief. That said, it would look way too unnatural if he walked outside with the pillow under his arm.

"Actually... Come to think of it, I bet nobody's open at this hour anyway."

The sky in the east had begun to pale a little, but it was still dark outside. Late night was just beginning to shift into early morning.

If this place had a manager, I could ask if there was a blanket I could borrow, but...

Suddenly, there was a knock. The door was decrepit, and the sound was louder than he'd expected in the small room. Nader felt as if something had clutched his heart.

"...! ...—!" Hastily hiding his pillow behind him, he held his breath, staring at the door.

Who's that?! There's no way I'd be getting a normal caller at this hour of the morning.

The door had a simple lock, which he'd used, but anybody who wanted to break it could do that pretty easily with a hammer. If this was one of Huey's underlings coming to bump him off, his luck would run out right here.

No, no way. To hell with that! You ain't gettin' me here, you bastards!

Still holding his breath, he turned back, looking at the window. This was the third floor, but maybe he could jump...

As Nader was wrapped in his panic, he heard a voice from beyond the door. It was more laid-back than he'd anticipated. "Hey, you okay in there? There was a really loud thud."

"......"

That had probably been him falling off the bed a minute ago. If the noise had traveled that well, it was best to assume everyone would hear everything.

"...Yeah, it's all jake. I just fell. Sorry if I woke you up."

"Nah, don't worry about it... Uh, I've got the room downstairs, but I also help manage this place. You just got in today, right? Lemme introduce myself."

"......"

What do I do? Is this a trap? But if I turn him down and he breaks the lock, it won't make a difference...

On top of that, if it turned out he was wrong, it would get harder to operate out of this place.

After a brief hesitation, Nader hid his pillow under the bed, then slowly unlocked the door.

He was relieved when he peeked through the crack and saw the face outside. This wasn't someone he knew, and he didn't seem too tough. He looked patently unhealthy, a type even Nader could probably knock down easily.

...? This fella looks like he's on the level now, but...I bet he used to be a junkie.

He had that unique pallor about him, but his eyes were clear and focused. He figured if the guy had been on dope before, he'd kicked the habit now. Nader opened the door wide and checked to see if anyone was behind him. Once it looked clear, he said, "I'm Goose. Who're you?"

Nader introduced himself by a random false name. The young man's hollow cheeks quirked in a smile, and he gave his own name.

"I'm Roy Maddock. If you run into any trouble, just let me know."

⇔

Several hours later   The lodging house dining hall

His incredibly brief nap seemed to have taken away a good bit of his drowsiness, because Nader never did manage to get to sleep.

When mouthwatering smells started to drift up to him, he remembered he hadn't eaten anything since noon the previous day, so he followed his nose, walking rather unsteadily.

The dining hall was in what looked like the old hotel's remodeled lobby, and a lot of people were already there. Most of them were residents, but there also seemed to be a few tramps who'd been hanging around nearby.

The smell of liquor hung in the air as well. A few diners were definitely already drunk.

Starting the morning with a drink in this economy?!

Still, some of the liquor stank like patently low-quality stuff, while other types smelled more like industrial or medical alcohol, so he decided not to think about it.

Where am I supposed to pay for this?

As Nader hesitated, unsure what to do, the assistant manager who'd come to his room earlier called to him. "Hi there, Goose. You just stayed up, huh?"

The other man had used the false name he'd given him earlier, and for a second, Nader wondered who he was talking to. Managing to keep his anxiety hidden, he forced a casual smile. "…Yeah, couldn't get back to sleep. Uh, Roy, wasn't it?"

"Yeah. For starters, breakfast here is free. It's included in your rent, see. Eat all you want." Roy brought over his own breakfast and Nader's, setting them down on a nearby table. "You're lucky; the dining hall's pretty empty this morning. I dunno what it was about, but there were airplanes flying around yesterday. Some folks were up into the small hours, hollering about how we'd gone to war and applesauce like that. Apparently, that bunch is still in bed."

"Really now? …Wait, free breakfast? That's pretty fine hospitality."

Come to think of it, they were passing out food until late last night, too.

It couldn't hurt to know more about the place where he was hiding out. Nader sat down next to Roy and asked for details. "Is the landlord that flush?"

"Well, he's a fine doctor. Apparently, he has more wealthy patients than you'd figure… He uses that money to see hard up fellas like us for cheap; it's real generous of him."

"He sounds like a pushover."

"I'm with you there. After all, he set a reformed dope addict like me up with a proper job. This lodging house is basically charity; about half the tenants were under his care before they settled down here." At that point, Roy paused to take a sip of milk from his mug, then went on. "It's not all the doc's money, though. There's a big mafia outfit in

Chicago that had local shopping districts cough up some money, then used it to openly run soup kitchens to win public support, you know? It's like that. Several of the local gangs make joint contributions to it."

"Joint contributions...?"

"It just goes to show how good our landlord's connections are. It's great for the gangs, too. This way, the starving citizens complain about the government, not them." Casually digging into his breakfast, Ray glanced at Nader's prosthetic hand. "Well, they can't provide food for several thousand people, like that big Chicago syndicate. Anyway, our doc's got a soft spot for folks who are sick or injured... Come to think of it, I wonder if the attendant let you move in without a fuss because he saw that fake hand of yours."

"...Oh. This thing?" Moving his prosthetic—although its fingers were fixed in place—Nader tapped it on the tabletop with a *thunk*. "Well, I'm pretty used to it by now."

"You've got it better than me. Sometimes the aftereffects of the dope make my whole body lock up. Still, I bet that hand makes it real hard to find work in times like these."

I knew it. This guy actually was a dope fiend, huh?

Sounds like he's cleaned up his act now, though.

Nader observed Roy absently, but the assistant manager was observing him right back. "There's that burn on your face, too. Was it some kind of accident?"

"!"

Dammit. I forgot and washed my face earlier.

Or maybe... That cold sweat might've washed it off way before that.

Nader had gotten his burns the time the Lemures' bomb had almost killed him. He'd miraculously made it out alive only because he'd used the bodies of his fellow traitors to shield himself, and he'd then been saved by a passing doctor who'd seen the blast. He hid the scars with makeup so Hilton and the other surviving Lemures wouldn't recognize him.

Come to think of it, other than Hilton, the Lemures only knew what he looked like without the burns. Would it be better not to hide them?

"I mean, if it's hard to talk about, you don't have to," Roy said.

Nader decided to tell a half-truth. He thought it was better to partially use the other man's goodwill, rather than clumsily keep the truth under wraps and make him suspicious. "Oh, nah, it's just… Way back when, I almost got killed by some mafia goons."

"Almost got killed… What, for real?"

"Yeah. Those fellas might still be after me. I'd rather word that there's a guy with burn scars and a fake hand staying here didn't get around."

"Hey, relax. Nobody at this place would do a thing like that."

"Can't be sure. If the mafia issued a bounty…" Even as he said it, he imagined what would happen if Hilton and the others actually put a bounty on him, and an awful chill ran through him.

However, Roy interpreted this as the reaction of a man running scared from the mob, and he tried to calm him down. "I'm telling you, it's fine. Anybody like that would get zotzed by the nastier types who hang out here, first thing."

"The nastier types?"

"It's like I said: The doc who runs this place is a pushover. Don't matter your race or how much money you got, he'll examine anybody."

So the guy's either a terrible hypocrite or he's got a few screws loose. Or maybe he's an actual hero type of guy…

He'd meant the idea to be ironic, but partway through, his thoughts turned self-deprecating. Reining in his mind, Nader responded casually. "…That's really something. And?"

"He doesn't care about race, age, sex, or how much money they've got or don't got, but that's not all. He's also not picky about what line of work they're in, or whether they're good or bad. He treats penniless junkies like me, and gangsters who got shot up in gunfights, and hitmen whose targets nailed them first—all of us equally." At that point, Roy glanced around, then smiled wryly and lowered his voice. "We've got quite a few fellas with pasts here. There's an unspoken rule that if you see somebody, you make like you didn't. If anybody turned stoolie in a place like this, well… You know what would happen, right?"

"…Yeah. I'll keep that in mind," Nader told him. Inwardly, he thought, *I see… My luck may have taken a turn for the better. After* all, Huey's underlings had plenty of cabbage. I doubt they'd come within a mile of a place like this. In a way, being able to hide among people who've got their own stuff to hide is a big help.

Gloating privately, Nader dug into his breakfast, holding his spoon in his left hand.

There wasn't much hamburger in the chili con carne, but the tomatoes and beans were pleasantly spicy, and the more he ate, the more his appetite woke up.

"...This is good."

"Ain't it, though?" Roy shrugged, smiling. Nader returned the smile, sincerely this time, and went on eating.

It was the first real meal he'd had as a free man.

It might have had a lot to do with his empty belly, but the taste was somehow soothing. It reminded him of his hometown.

......?

He'd assumed the doctor who'd fed him was a hypocrite and missing a few screws. Who the hell did he think he was? Nader felt something like self-loathing—and it surprised him quite a lot.

He'd betrayed all sorts of people up till now. The fact that he could feel self-loathing over such a minor thing after everything was ridiculous.

Maybe too much had happened since then.

Everything about the life he'd lived had proven worthless, and his past was haunting him with such a vengeance that he couldn't hope to run.

The fear of being pursued had put a collar on him. He'd become a slave to his own karma.

He really must have taken a wrong turn somewhere.

I... Why...? Where...?

His regrets circled around and around until it felt like he was losing the ability to think anything else. Realizing this was bad news, Nader decided to distract himself by focusing on his breakfast.

That's right. For now, I can relax here.

This place is the newest one I've managed to make it to. That means my past hasn't gotten here yet.

Repeating this silently in his mind, Nader kept working on his chili con carne.

*   *   *

...But he'd forgotten a few things.

First, that he hadn't yet tried to throw all his strength behind anything, even making an escape.

Second, he'd come to this town not by running away but through a current taking him there.

If he'd been pulled into the strange whirlpools that surrounded the immortals even marginally—in the end, he'd be washed to the same place they were.

Since he hadn't struggled to escape the vortex, he was approaching a certain fate—one that was extremely close to coincidence but could still have been called *inevitable*.

"Man... This is real good stuff."

"Tell it to the guy who's working the kitchen today." Roy laughed at Nader, who was sounding like a broken record. "The breakfast cook is another fella who got hurt for reasons he can't talk about. He cooks here in the mornings, then works during the day. He said he was saving up so he could become some kind of musician."

"Huh. So he's keeping his nose to the grindstone."

"Sounds like it... Well, speak of the devil. Here he comes now." Roy put up a hand toward someone behind Nader. "Hey, c'mon over. Let me introduce you to the new fella."

In response, Nader heard a sigh from somewhere behind him.

"What's this 'introducing the new fella' business? Folks move in and move out every day; this isn't like you, Roy."

"Well, this particular new fella says he likes your cooking."

"Say, thanks, pal. I'm glad you're happy about it." In response to Roy's explanation, the breakfast cook thanked him politely.

I should probably at least look him in the face when I say hi, right? On that thought, Nader slowly turned around. At almost the same moment, Roy said his name.

"Let me introduce you. This is Mr. Goose."

At that point, right in the middle of his turn, he froze.

......

...Oh yeah. My fake name.

It was the pseudonym he'd introduced himself by earlier. Even though he'd been in the dining hall for only a few minutes, he'd almost forgotten it again, and he told himself to get it together already.

I shouldn't have picked "Goose," huh...

It really had been a mistake to use the name of the direct superior who'd almost killed him, Nader mused as he started to turn again.

Just then, Roy spoke to the breakfast cook; he sounded perplexed. "What's the matter? Why so startled, Upham?"

Upham.

When he heard that name, Nader froze.

"Oh, no, it's just, my old boss had the same name." The breakfast cook was laughing cheerfully, but his voice gave Nader a nasty premonition.

At this point, Nader couldn't tell if that voice was familiar. He wasn't confident he could place it against voices he'd heard a while back. He'd always planned to betray his comrades and use them as stepping-stones, and he'd never tried to remember their voices.

However, he did remember the name "Upham"—and that guy had said his old boss had been named Goose.

The bad feeling made Nader's spine stiff with tension.

Should he run or try to bluff it out?

In the moment he hesitated, the situation got worse.

"...Huh?"

Upham, who'd come up beside the table, saw his profile and frowned.

"Say... Are you Nader?"

It's all over.

That was the sole phrase running through Nader's mind. In the end, he'd played himself.

Why... Why is this guy here?!

He'd seen the breakfast cook's face out of the corner of his eye, and he did recognize him.

The young guy had been a Lemures underling who'd spent his

spare moments looking at Chané. He'd seemed timid, so Nader had figured he'd be easily led, which was why he'd brought up the "sellout" with him pretty early on. However, in the end, Nader was the one who'd been sold out, and he'd lost both his right hand and his foothold in life.

Nader would have been lying if he'd said he wasn't holding a grudge, but he was beyond caring about details like that right now. The one thing he knew for sure was the temporary sense of relief he'd felt when he started on his breakfast had vanished like the mirage it was.

In an instant, Nader had swapped the spoon in his left hand for a fork and lunged at Upham, bolting from his chair with enough force to knock it over.

"Hey!"

By the time Roy's voice echoed in the dining hall, Nader had already pinned Upham from behind and shoved the tines of the fork against his neck. Steeling himself to run it into Upham's throat, Nader asked him a tense question. "...Did Hilton send you here to kill me?" If he'd given it a little thought, he would have realized that didn't mesh with what Roy had told him, but in the moment, he couldn't see Upham as anything but a Lemure assassin.

Naturally, Upham had only realized the other guy was Nader a moment earlier, so the whole situation was a complete shock to him. "Huh?! C-calm down! Look, Nader, how are you even alive?!" he asked, confused.

Teeth chattering, Nader shouted at him. "Don't play dumb with me! There's no way one of the Lemures would be hanging around a place like this if Hilton hadn't sent them!" Nader was the one threatening his opponent at forkpoint, and he clearly had the advantage, but he was far more frightened than Upham.

By this point, Upham picked up on the fact that Nader wasn't thinking clearly. "Wait! I'm not with the Lemures anymore! I quit ages back! Forget me—what's your deal?! Why are you here, using Master Goose's name...?!" he said in desperation.

"Put a cork in it!" Nader barked. He was already struggling to

process the situation, and he didn't have the spare brainpower to answer the other guy's questions. He had no idea what to do next. He just stood there, in full view of the whole dining hall.

"Okay, okay, just put the fork down, Goose... Or, uh, Nader? Whichever." Roy put his hands up, trying to talk Nader down. "There's no fighting here. I dunno what happened between you fellas way back when, but while you're living at this place, forget about the past. None of that means anything here. I'll do you no wrong, and Upham won't, either. You get that, right?"

"......"

Even though Nader was breathing roughly, he looked Roy in the eye. Then he fell silent.

He had Upham locked in place, but he had no plan beyond that. Would it be safer to kill the guy and head right back to the clink? His paranoia was starting to make him think so. Gradually, he put more force behind the fork at Upham's throat.

"H-hey, Nader, stop! Don't do it!" Upham practically screamed, and Nader tried to yell at him to shut up. However, those words were forced back down into his throat when he felt something cold grind against his temple.

It was the muzzle of a large-caliber gun.

Nader's breath hitched. From beside him, a man quietly said, "Starting a standoff with a fork as a weapon. You're a lunatic, fella."

"...Ah...agh..."

Nader's mouth flapped uselessly. The man who was holding a shotgun to his head kept talking; there was a sharp look in his eyes. "I don't hate your insanity, but it's nowhere near enough to hinder my own lunacy. Don't fill the dining hall with your terrified thirst for blood. You'll lower the purity of mine."

The man with the shotgun wasn't making sense. Next to him, a boy with blond hair and a young face gave him a sidelong glance. "Couldn't you just say what you mean and tell him not to interrupt your breakfast, Master?"

"Quiet, Apprentice One."

*   *   *

As he listened to this exchange, Nader felt sticky sweat break out all over his body. Death was staring him in the face.

Not only that, but if he trusted what he'd heard, this had nothing to do with Hilton or the Lemures. This was all because he disturbed somebody's meal.

This isn't funny. I haven't been running pathetically all this time just to die here over something like this!

He felt like crying, but the terror of the gun against his temple made his whole body freeze, and even his tear ducts didn't seem to be working. His eyes were getting drier by the second. He couldn't stab the fork into Upham's throat, and he couldn't throw it away, either. He was petrified, as if a curse had turned him to stone.

"Mr. Smith, don't you antagonize him, either! Put the gun away, all right?! That thing's no joke!" Roy yelled.

Smith shook his head. His expression was cold. "Listen. If I'm going to sheathe my insanity once drawn, there are two things that must be respected. One is the world, which still permits me, the vessel of insanity, to exist. The other..."

The man was monologuing with his fancy words like a regular poetaster. All Nader could do was listen, but then a powerful stench of alcohol surrounded them.

"...?"

An old man had appeared next to him, on the other side from Smith and his gun. His face was flushed, and he was making no attempt to hide the boozy smell.

"At leash...lemme drink my likker in peace. 'Kay, bo?" The old man took a gulp straight from the bottle of whiskey he was holding. Nader didn't have time to deal with a drunk, and he started to turn his attention back to Smith—

—when a heavy blow struck his face.

For a second, he thought he'd been shot, but there was no way he would have been conscious after such a thing. He didn't understand it, but the pain warped his vision. He fumbled the fork and crumpled to the dining hall floor as if his strings had been cut.

*   *   *

"…Hey, alki. I was talking."

"Your tomfool speechifying makes my poor, hungover head throb."

The reeking drunk had slammed his whiskey bottle into Nader's face, and now he and the man with the shotgun were facing off over his fallen body.

"And anyway," the drunk continued, "a fella who tried to take out both the Gandors and his own comrades in a surprise attack ain't got no right to say any of that."

"Why you… You're bringing that up now? Besides, that Mexican girl was hardly a comrade."

Smith was clearly in a bad mood, but the old man didn't seem to care. "I remember it like it was yesterday. That big ol' scar on your face is proof they got you instead." He snorted and took another swig from his bottle.

The geezer's attitude made Smith's temples twitch, but the blond kid and Roy separated them.

As he watched the exchange play out above him, Nader felt himself slipping away, on the verge of blacking out. *C'mon… What is this? They're not gonna finish me off?*

Neither the man with the gun nor the old drunk were paying him any mind, as if his presence didn't even register to them anymore.

At that point, Nader was finally convinced those two weren't assassins. Then Roy's voice echoed in his ears. "Hey, you okay, Goose? Uh, Nader?"

"Yeesh. I don't even get what you got wrong. You alive down there?" Even Upham checked up on him. He was rubbing his throat.

Oh, I knew it. Realizing he'd become a total clown, Nader broke into a smile. *No matter how hard I struggle, I guess I can't be a hero.*

Then he blacked out completely.

Having been forced to see his own weakness, he was practically running away out of sheer embarrassment.

Or he was turning his eyes as far as he could from the fact that he'd never be a hero, no matter how he tried.

Chapter 11   All the Players Are in Place but Not on the Same Page

Millionaires' Row

Half a day had passed since the ruckus at the Martillo Family gambling den. Dawn had broken.

When the gang of delinquents who were living at the Genoard family's second residence woke up and gathered in the hall, a bizarre sight greeted them.

"…What is this?"

Everybody reacted the same way and then stopped in their tracks.

"Why are you all standing there like statues? …What is this?" On his way to the kitchen to get breakfast started, Fang Lin-Shan peeked into the hall. He, too, came to a stop.

He'd seen a row of neatly folded tuxedos and tailcoats, and a large variety of evening gowns on hangers.

A special rack that held about a dozen gowns stood in the center of the room. That startled him first, but more than anything, the quality and quantity of the garments completely floored him.

Even though they were smack in the middle of a recession, the classy formalwear didn't show the faintest sign of shoddy manufacturing. The cloth was luxurious, the elegant styles had a sophisticated feel, and the fabric had that special "new" scent. The garments certainly didn't look out of place in the Genoard family's second residence on Millionaires' Row—but the delinquents who currently occupied the mansion had never expected to encounter anything like them.

"Um…"

The hall had been transformed into a modest high-class clothing boutique. However, what confused them even more was the sight of Jacuzzi Splot sitting in a corner of it, hugging his knees.

"Jacuzzi? Jacuzzi, what's the matter?"

"Did a traveling salesman come through and strong-arm you into buying all these threads?"

"No… Nobody could carry all that around by themselves."

"I woke up early, and when I walked past this room six thousand twenty-seven seconds ago, there wasn't the hint of a ghost of this pile of clothes."

"Actually, did you lug all these in on your own, Jacuzzi?"

"Nwah, Jacuzzi, you muscleman."

"Hya-haah?" "Hya-haw!"

His friends kept talking to him, but Jacuzzi didn't respond. He just heaved a deep sigh, his arms still around his knees. He was somehow depressed and half asleep at the same time.

They hadn't been able to pay their protection money to the Martillo Family, and so Jacuzzi had gone out to beg for work. He'd returned without anyone noticing—and now this.

The delinquents didn't try to shake Jacuzzi awake to find out what happened. Instead, they started taking random guesses.

"Mgaw… Jacuzzi, you get job?"

"Is this the job? Selling these off?"

"But who's gonna buy 'em in this recession?"

"…Maybe Miss Eve?"

"There's no point in selling her tuxedos—or dresses for grown-up ladies."

"Are we selling them to that Dallas git? To him, huh?"

"If he had any other fat-cat connections, he'd already be trying them."

"Hya-haah!"

While some of the delinquents interpreted the clothes as merchandise, another group decided they were contraband.

"I see, Jacuzzi... You were flat broke, so you finally went and did it, huh?"

"Uh... I dunno, fella. Stealing clothes from a store run by regular folks isn't a great move."

"If your back was really against the wall, you shoulda said somethin'. We would have helped."

"And hey, where are we supposed to unload these?"

"Hya-haw."

The boys and girls went on shooting their mouths off, but Jacuzzi didn't respond.

It was as if he was trying to run away from reality by staying asleep.

"What's all the fuss about in...here?"

Nice walked in, then looked as startled as the rest of them. Listening to the conversations around her and deciding nobody else knew anything, she shook Jacuzzi awake.

"Jacuzzi, Jacuzzi! Wake up! Pull yourself together! What happened?!"

"Nn......huh? Uwaaaugh?! Nice?! Uh, huh? Did I fall asleep?"

"You looked like you were having some kind of nightmare. What on earth happened?" Nice asked.

Jacuzzi took a hasty look around the room. When he saw all the formal clothes, his lips trembled wretchedly. "Aaaaaaaaaaaaaah, I knew it... I knew it wasn't a dreeeeeam."

"Calm down, Jacuzzi. What are these clothes for? Where did you get them?"

"Huh...? Oh... Um, well..."

Nice rubbed his shoulders gently, and it seemed to soothe him. Little by little, Jacuzzi calmed down. However, for some reason, the calmer he was, the paler he got. "What'll I do? Those clothes... I want to explain, but now that I'm really thinking about it, I stuck my foot into something incredibly awful..."

"What do you mean?"

"Th-the clothes are, um… They're a loan."

"A loan? …From whom?"

Nice prioritized the question of "From whom?" over "What for?" Knowing the name would let her gauge the depth of the swamp Jacuzzi had stumbled into.

"The Martillo Family, or technically…from Mr. Ronny."

The swamp was practically bottomless, as it happened.

Nice froze, but Jacuzzi went on anyway, explaining the despair that awaited them.

"And so…we're all going to wear these and help out at a mafia gambling den…"

⇔

A few hours earlier

"Hey… I think I recognize that tattoo."

"Aaaah! I—I'msorryexcusemeforgiveme!" The kid with the inked face shrieked and scrambled back in a dramatic show of terror.

Firo frowned. "Uh, why are you apologizing?"

"I—I'm sorry, I'm really sorry!"

"What I mean is, *quit* apologizing."

"Eep! I—I'm s— Um, no, I…I—I—I won't apologize, so please forgive me!"

The kid was panicking like a small animal who'd seen a fire. Firo thought, *What is this girly little…? Geez, he's so timid that calling him "girly" would be an insult to women.* He didn't let his feelings show on his face, though. Instead, he asked him another question. "Uh… We've met a few times before, haven't we? Several years back. You came limping off that train…and you were on the top floor of Mist Wall, too, right?"

"Y-you saw me there?!"

"I heard about you from Ronny. You're the… What was it…? The leader of those delinquent kids, and your name is…uh…"

"J-Jacuzzi. I'm Jacuzzi Splot."

Mist Wall was one thing, but Jacuzzi hadn't known he'd been seen leaving the Flying Pussyfoot. The other guy seemed terribly well-informed, and that did nothing to settle his nerves.

"Gotcha. I'm Firo. Good to meet you, Jacuzzi. So what are you doing in a place like this? Not only that, but it looks like you know Ladd…"

Firo shot Ladd a sidelong glance, but he had calmed down and was talking with Graham and Lua. He didn't seem to be paying attention to Firo's conversation.

"I—I, um… The Russo Family put a bounty on me… Then on the train, Ladd put me off until later, and then Mr. Molsa told me to go with Ronny, so I did, but Ladd was here…" Jacuzzi's fear seemed to have confused him more, and he couldn't describe what had happened properly. Completely failing to give anything resembling an explanation, he put on his very best social smile and finished with "And so we're in your hands, so please go easy on us!"

Silence fell as Firo narrowed his eyes. "…What the hell are you talking about?"

"Eep!" Jacuzzi was as stiff as a board.

Oh, sh-sh-sh-shoot. H-he didn't get any of that! Jacuzzi panicked. *I—I mean, I don't understand why Ladd is here…! A-and this man… He knows both Ladd and that scary red-eyed guy?! What's up with that?!*

Not only was this baby-faced man friends with Ladd and Christopher, he had Ronny Schiatto and Molsa Martillo behind him. He looked around Jacuzzi's age, but as far as Jacuzzi was concerned, he might as well be Satan, served by all the devils in hell.

H-huh? But… Come to think of it, I've heard the name "Firo" before. I get the feeling Isaac and Miria mentioned him a lot.

"Um… Do you know Isaac and Miria?" Jacuzzi asked.

"Huh? What about them? …Actually, I seem to remember asking *you* a question. What's with the third degree, huh?" Firo's eyes hardened, and his expression was impossible to read.

"Waaaaaugh, I—I'm sorry! Really, I'm sorry! Please don't kill me!"

"Look, I told you, quit apologizing over peanuts!" Firo was getting nowhere with Jacuzzi. Sighing, he called to Ronny. "Ronny, who the hell is this guy?"

"Hmm… You delay the introduction of your own acquaintances but demand I introduce Jacuzzi. Emotionally, you seem to be stretched very thin. Well, no matter."

"…Sorry." Firo had forgotten he'd said that. His own blunder irritated him.

"I told you it didn't matter. Don't apologize so easily," Ronny said.

"……" Firo snapped his mouth shut, embarrassed to hear his own words used against him.

Ronny's lips curved in a smirk. "I'm joking. Don't let it bother you… In any case, I am the one who brought Jacuzzi Splot, Rail, Ricardo Russo, and Christopher Shaldred here."

One of those Ronny had just named spoke up. "Huh? Did I ever tell him my full name?" Christopher said.

"It doesn't matter," Ricardo replied, tugging on the tail of his jacket. Christopher fell silent.

Watching them out of the corner of his eye, Ronny went on. "They're here to help you with your job, Firo."

"Huh?" Firo had been listening obediently, but at that last remark, he looked up. "No, uh, Ronny… These guys are supposed to— What again?"

"There's a certain event coming up in the middle of February. I'm going to have them help you there. There are actually a lot more of them, including Jacuzzi's companions. Rail over there, to begin with."

"…What?!"

The "certain event" was probably the casino opening hosted by the Runorata Family, the group that had dropped in a minute ago. Firo had assumed it was just a political maneuver on their part.

However, Melvi had been the spitting image of Maiza's kid brother, and seeing him had forced Firo to rethink the entire situation. *These guys? Help me out? A whiny weakling, some kids...and Christopher?! C'mon!*

"It's all right, Ronny. I can run the place just fine without helpers," Firo insisted.

He actually thought they'd be in the way, but he didn't say so out loud. Ronny had brought them, and he didn't want to insult a superior in front of strangers.

Ronny knew exactly what Firo meant, though. "You look as if you imagine they'll be in the way."

"N-no... That's not what I..." As Firo tried to cover for himself, Christopher stuck his oar in from behind him.

"That's mean, Firo! I just wanted to be useful to you, since you were my first friend here in the city!" Even as Christopher protested, he was wearing a smirk.

This conversation was giving Firo a headache, but Firo didn't ignore him. "Frankly, I don't trust you. You look like you'd shoot up the casino."

"Wow. That's incredible! You know me really well! A true-blue friend to the end!"

"Oh, shut up."

As he watched the pair, Jacuzzi felt a little relieved.

Oh, good. If Firo thinks we'll be in the way, we might not have to do anything dangerous. But then we'll need to think of some other way to make money...

While Jacuzzi was lost in thought, Firo had gotten fed up with Christopher and stopped mincing words. "C'mon, Ronny, what can these guys actually do? I know Christopher's good in a fight, but the rest of 'em are just kids."

"Oh yeah? They look about the same age as you, Firo," Christopher said, cackling.

Firo shot him his sharpest look yet and issued a warning. "...Say that one more time, and I'll file all your teeth down to your gums."

If Maiza and the others hadn't been right there, he might have skipped straight to throwing punches.

"I—I'm sorry!"

However, the one who apologized was Jacuzzi, not Christopher. Firo had looked so menacing that Jacuzzi couldn't help it. He was shaking like a leaf.

"...Again, why are you apologizing?" Firo snapped.

"Eep!" Jacuzzi squeaked like a baby rat who'd attracted the cat's attention. Tears were forming in his eyes.

What's with this guy? Firo grumbled silently. *Can't imagine him having the guts to get inked on his face. What, did some bullies come after him? Did they pin him down for that tattoo?*

Firo frowned. "...Ronny, this really isn't gonna cut it. I can't see this spineless crybaby doing anything for us. Besides, his friends are probably all—"

"Firo." Maiza started to warn Firo to watch his tongue, but Ronny stopped him with a gesture.

"Firo Prochainezo."

"...?! Y-yessir?"

Ronny's quiet voice made Firo freeze. Not only had Ronny called him by his full name, but his usual imperturbable smile had vanished, and his face was perfectly expressionless.

"Say any more, and you'll be insulting our *capo masto* along with the boy."

"Huh...?"

"He was the one who decided they would be useful to you," Ronny explained. "Showing contempt for them is questioning his judgment. Am I wrong?"

"......"

Ronny's impassive remark left Firo speechless. Molsa Martillo was the law in Firo's mind. If the head of the Martillo Family had acknowledged these guys, then doubting their capabilities was tantamount to betrayal.

"...I'm very sorry, sir," Firo said, directing his apology both at

Ronny and the absent Molsa from the bottom of his heart. Then Firo turned to Jacuzzi and gave him a sincere apology as well. "Sorry to you, too, fella. I came pretty close to insulting your friends. Forgive me."

"Huh? Oh, erm…" The terrifying man had apologized to him, and Jacuzzi had no idea how to react other than with his usual timidity. A strange silence fell over the room.

Ricardo, whom Firo hadn't paid much attention to, was the one who broke it. "It's only natural to worry about how the work may go, judging only by our appearances and our behavior here. We don't want to shame Mr. Martillo's name, either, and we'll give the job everything we have. I'd appreciate it if you'd judge us based on our performance."

Ricardo spoke smoothly, without any reticence toward Firo.

And then there's this kid. He's really got it together, Firo thought, amazed. "Y-yeah… Okay."

Ricardo seemed a heck of a lot more like an adult than Firo felt. He was just feeling daunted by that when Ladd chimed in from across the room.

"You'd never think we were related, wouldja? It startled me, too." Ladd laughed. Then his eyes went to Jacuzzi. "I'll also vouch for Tattoo Boy's moxie. After all, he was the biggest bounty on the Russo Family's list. When I messed with his friend a little, he looked me straight in the eye, and you know what he said? 'We'll make you pay for this.'"

"……!" Trembling, Jacuzzi gasped and gave an inarticulate shriek.

Firo watched him, and his eyes said he still didn't believe it. Still, Ladd probably wasn't the type who'd joke about a thing like that.

As if for good measure, the guy in the blue coveralls who stood beside Ladd interjected loudly, spinning his enormous wrench. "Let me tell you a sad, sad story. It seems to me as if my sworn kid brother Jacuzzi is being unfairly underrated… You, Ladd's friend: I'm gonna list a hundred of Jacuzzi's good points right now. If I run out, I'll have to imagine his future exploits and work with those instead. Ready?!"

"Nah," Firo said. "That sounds like it would take forever, so I'll pass."

Genuinely shocked, the one with the wrench screamed at a young man who appeared to be his henchman. "How can this be?! He shot me down! Inconceivable! What do I do, Shaft?! I feel like my reason for existing just got rejected. What am I supposed to do now?!"

The henchman heaved a sigh, sounding worn out. "You could probably just shut up."

"Okay, got it! I'll shut up! However, I want to tell everybody here just one thing! If I were you, I wouldn't underestimate Jacuzzi. If you underestimate him, worst-case scenario...you'll die."

"No, they won't!! Actually, I'm the one who'd die!"

The yelped retort came from none other than Jacuzzi himself. His statement seemed to have shocked Wrench Guy yet again, and he gestured emotionally with the enormous tool. "That's insane... He says he's the one who'd die... You mean you'd take on the fate of those who underestimate you and die in their place?! Damn, fella, just how nice are you?! And how brave! What do we call someone so kind and brave? How should I describe Jacuzzi?! A hero, perhaps? Yeah, a hero. There could be no other word!"

"No, um..."

I don't want people overestimating me..., Jacuzzi thought. As the conversation got bigger and bigger, he couldn't keep up with it. He felt as if something dreadful would happen if this went on, and he started thinking of ways to deny the evaluation.

The time for that had already passed, though.

Firo, who'd eyed him dubiously at first, gave him a firm nod. "I don't really get what that guy in the coveralls is saying, but it looks like you've got the respect of quite a few people. Trust from others is a powerful weapon. I'll expect great things from you, Jacuzzi Splot."

"No, erm..."

"You don't have to be so jumpy. After all, if anything happens, I'm the one who'll take the fall."

W-was this that big a deal?!

That only made Jacuzzi feel more pressured. Thinking it was

extremely bad news that he still didn't know what sort of job he'd be doing this late in the game, he asked him about it, partly to change the subject. "Um... Specifically what do you want us to do on the day? Mr. Molsa said we'd only have to gamble, but..."

When Firo heard that, he nodded as if it made sense. "I see, It sounds like the *capo masto* is planning to have you be *risacca*."

"R-*risacca*?"

"It's a slang term our family uses. Other outfits have different names for it, but... It's a unique job, not quite like being a plant..." Firo thought for a little, then explained, doing his best to choose words that would be easy to understand. "Basically, you act like incoming waves, *bringing the right mood to the place*. You boost the level of excitement, or sometimes bring it down, so that people will want to raise their bets. It's a job that regulates the mood of the whole casino. It's not cheating or anything. It's just that having the right mood is important, see.

"In a way, it's a more important role than dealer or my job running the place. Thanks in advance for your help, Jacuzzi Splot."

⇔

The present   Millionaires' Row

"...So you see, between now and the job, we have to learn how to gamble at casinos, etiquette, and all sorts of other things. Mr. Ronny said he'd lend us all these clothes. I don't know how he did it, but by the time I got back here, they were sitting in the hall..."

Jacuzzi explained the situation absently, gazing at the ceiling and definitely not at Nice.

From his jacket pocket, he took out the note he'd found in the entryway when he got back.

By the day of the casino job, at the very latest, we need you to be able to conduct yourselves like the rich. I'll lend you formalwear, so accustom yourselves to it. Gang executives and the wealthy won't be easily influenced by town thugs, no matter how much noise they make.

I expect great things from you.

Oh, yes. As an advance, I've temporarily paid your protection money for this month and the next, on your behalf.

Ronny Schiatto

After showing everyone the note, Jacuzzi looked as though his soul had been extracted:

"…In other words," he murmured, "it's too late to back out."

And so the delinquents of Millionaires' Row were dragged completely into the whirlpool.

None of them were immortals or mafiosi. However, simply because there were some in close proximity, they'd gotten swept into the maelstrom. It pulled in the whirlpools from their own lives right along with them, expanding further.

Thus, the human chain went on, whether destined for tragedy or comedy.

At the point, yet another drifting soul who'd been drawn into the huge vortex generated by the Runorata Family and the immortals appeared to Jacuzzi's group.

Nice wasn't trying to avert her eyes from the hopeless situation that confronted her, but before she touched on the subject of the casino, she asked about something that had been on her mind for a little while. "By the way, where's Rail?"

It was a simple question but an important one, and Jacuzzi answered it easily. "Oh, she met up with some old friends, so she said she'd spend the evening at their place…"

Then they heard a noise from the entryway.

"I wonder if Rail's back."

Jacuzzi and the others headed for the front entrance en masse—but the person they found there wasn't Rail. It was a familiar face a few years older than they were.

"Hey. You bottom-feeders look as broke as ever."

The man who'd appeared, talking like a man with a worse upbringing than anyone present, was—in a way—their landlord.

"Da...Dallas?!"

Eve Genoard was the current head of the Genoard family.

This guy was her big brother, but he hadn't inherited the family fortune. He was a typical good-for-nothing who sold off the family's antiques and paintings and spent all his time playing around.

He was disparaging toward Jacuzzi's group, but he was disparaging toward all of humanity—with the exception of his little sister. They knew him too well to get mad at him for it.

Unaware that Jacuzzi and the others were watching him with a sort of pity in their eyes, Dallas leered at them. He might as well have been the representative of all vulgar thugs. "I've got a good offer for you scumbags today."

He had a remark of his own that would plunge him into the giant whirlpool at his feet.

"Did you know they're holding a casino event at that Ra's Lance building in February?"

Chapter 12   The Quiet Man Doesn't Lose His Cool

Somewhere in New York   The basement of Coraggioso, a jazz hall

"It might get rough, huh?" muttered Berga Gandor, one of the Gandor Family's top executives. His younger brother, Luck, had just given him a report.

Once his initial surprise went away, Berga grinned. "Well, hey, bring it on. Hell, that building looks flimsy. Let's crush it and them both."

The jazz hall was run by the Gandor Family, one of New York's small mafia outfits. However, their office was in its basement, and in practical terms, it was their headquarters.

In a room in its depths, Luck Gandor—one of the three brothers who ran the syndicate—had just reported the events of the previous night. Although he'd pulled an all-nighter, he showed no sign of drowsiness. Instead, he gave them an extremely logical summary of what had happened at Firo's casino and what they could predict from that information.

"Let's grab all the roscoes we can find, starting now! The only pain would be running out of slugs! I mean, c'mon, there's a lotta Runoratas!" In sharp contrast to his coolheaded younger brother, Berga was filling the room with promises of violence.

"Calm down, Berga." Reprimanding his middle brother, Luck went on talking to Keith, the oldest. "The elixir of immortality seems to be involved here. However, Firo's attitude toward that Melvi fellow was... How should I put it...? A little odd. The man was normal at first, but as he was leaving, he passed Maiza. Maiza said something, and in that moment, his expression changed."

"What? That Melvi fella is Maiza's friend?" Berga asked.

Luck shook his head. "No... From what I saw later, that didn't appear to be the case... There may be some history between them, though. Something to do with the immortals."

"Like it matters whether it's about immortals or not. If they try to rumble with us, we'll stomp 'em flat—that's all! Right, Keith?!"

"......"

Keith was listening to his younger brothers' conversation in silence. However, his eyes were as sharp as well-honed knives, and a glare from them would have been enough to petrify an ordinary thug. He didn't express an opinion, but the intimidation he was radiating overawed Berga, who dialed it down on reflex. "Hey, whoa, don't look so scary, Keith. I get it, all right? I'll hear him out all the way to the end."

Luck chose that moment to scold his brother further. "The business about immortality is a fairy tale, Berga. Even if that's why we're getting dragged into a fight, we won't have an excuse to give the other organizations if we go to war with the Runoratas."

"...This sounds like a pain in the ass."

"It could be worse. Big syndicates can't even avenge their own without permission."

In America at the time, after Al Capone's arrest, whole organizations had decided to go underground. As a result, there were strong horizontal connections between syndicates, and a network known as Cosa Nostra, run by charismatic big-time gangsters, was growing larger than ever before.

Trouble between outfits was strictly monitored. In some cases, even if a member of a syndicate was killed, the syndicate had to get permission from the surrounding organizations before they made his killer pay the blood price. In the midst of that situation, while gangs that had always been powerful, like the Runoratas, were one thing, it was extremely unusual for small outfits, like the Gandors and the Martillos, to hold on to their places in Manhattan.

"On the other hand, I doubt the Runoratas want to quarrel with New York's Five Families, either. While things may very well get rough, I think they'll keep it below the surface. Neither we nor they have made pacts with any other mafia outfits. If either of us draws too much attention, we'll be targeted by the police. The Bureau of Investigation hates the very sight of the mafia. No doubt they'd like to crush any likely-looking target and move on from there."

"......"

Turning his head from Luck, who was going on and on, to Keith, who stayed silent, Berga ground his teeth. "Then what are we supposed to do, huh?!"

"We'll just have to ride it out with the cards in our hand. That's what we've always done... Including the last time we tangled with the Runoratas," Luck said, looking away slightly.

He was harboring a worry he didn't want the others to see.

"The cards in our hand," hmm? Our greatest blunder...is that the Runoratas have Claire, our joker.

Luck was going to have to tell his brothers about that, and he wasn't looking forward to it.

Their childhood friend had gone over to the enemy. Worse, they'd lost the most powerful card they knew of, which ensured that their position would be weak.

However, Luck was aware he couldn't just keep quiet about it, so he steeled himself. "By the way, there's one more important matter."

"......" "Huh? Well, spit it out."

Prompted by his brothers' gazes, Luck began to explain. "That Melvi fellow has a troublesome bodyguard..."

Just then, there was a knock at the door.

"Boss, got a minute?"

The voice belonged to a man who'd been on standby in the office.

They'd told him they were in a meeting, so if he was interrupting, it was probably something urgent.

"What is it?" As Luck spoke, he put on the hard-boiled mask he showed everyone but his brothers.

Timidly, the man made his report. "Uh, you've got a guest... He says he's a messenger from the Runorata Family. What should I tell him?"

The brothers exchanged glances.

"Is he alone?"

"No, uh, he's got a bodyguard with him..."

The word *bodyguard* sent a warning through Luck's mind. The complicated expression on the messenger's face transformed that hunch into certainty. Before Luck could say anything, his suspicions were confirmed.

"And that bodyguard is... Uh, he's somebody you know, boss."

A minute passed, and then the visitors walked in.

"Hey, it's been a while. For Keith and Berga anyway. For you, Luck, it's...what, about six hours? You don't look so great. Did you not sleep or something?" Claire—Felix—was wearing a gleaming, healthy-looking smile.

Luck put his index fingers against his temples. "If my color isn't good, it's because of you, Felix." Then, glaring at him through half-closed eyes, he outlined the situation rather ironically. "I was just about to tell Keith and Berga about this."

Then Luck turned his gaze to the fearlessly smiling man behind Claire.

Melvi greeted them with a courteous bow. His expression was the same one he'd worn the day before.

It wasn't clear whether Claire was paying attention to the guy behind him. He responded to Luck's sarcasm nonchalantly. "Oh yeah, that's right. Sorry 'bout this, Keith and Berga. The Runoratas hired me. In other words, depending on how things pan out, I could end up being your enemy."

"......"

Apparently, Keith had suspected as much from the moment they walked in together, because he said nothing.

In contrast, Berga yelled, his veins bulging. "What the—?! Claire, you bastard, what the hell is this?! There's no way you don't know what it's like between us and the Runoratas!"

"Well, hold the phone. I got hired by that big palooka Gustavo once before, remember? Even if it was just to track somebody down. Besides, you don't have a beef with the Runoratas right this minute. Also, it's Felix, not Claire."

Claire's reply was terribly irresponsible, and this time Berga was the one rubbing his temples. "Tch... Dammit, you're as impossible to predict as ever!"

"Well, if a fella like you read my moves, Berga, I think I might be all washed up as a human being."

"......Ha!"

"Ha! Ha! Ha!"

For a moment, they laughed at each other, and then—

Berga took a swing at Claire, and the childhood pals launched themselves into a ferocious brawl.

"Once they start, it takes a bit before they're finished. This way, please."

Ignoring the other two, who were flipping tables and tearing up the place, Luck invited Melvi into the small room they used for meetings.

"Are you sure you don't need to stop *that*?" Melvi glanced at the fight.

"We're used to it," Luck told him indifferently. "Don't worry about your security, either. If we were to turn a gun or a knife on you with lethal intent, even in the middle of his fight, he'd do something about it."

"You seem to have an extraordinary amount of trust for Felix."

"Both as an enemy and an ally, there aren't many people whose abilities are as trustworthy as his... Provided you set aside his character issues for the moment." Luck wasn't joking; he meant that sincerely.

"Is he trustworthy as a friend you've known since childhood?"

"I'm not partial to using the word *trust* as a gauge for old friends."

Restraining each other with words, Keith, Luck, and their guest Melvi sat down at a round table.

Luck took another close look at Melvi, but there didn't seem to be anything strange about the man. He didn't have the tough-guy exterior or the unique air of intimidation that denizens of the underworld tended to have. However, his very mildness was unsettling.

Well, if you only go from appearances, Firo doesn't look like a Camorra executive... And I can't really talk about others.

In contrast, Keith had the sharp air of an obvious mafia big-timer, while Berga looked like a classic fighter. Envying his brothers, Luck broached the main topic. "And? What are you plotting, Melvi?"

"...Plotting? That's a bold word to use at a first meeting."

"I believe we met at the Martillo Family's casino yesterday evening."

"We didn't speak." Apparently, he *had* noticed Luck. Melvi kept a smile on his face, but from experience, Luck guessed that smile was there to hide what he really felt.

"I beg your pardon. You did speak with Firo Prochainezo, the manager of that casino. From what I saw of that exchange, I feel I must view anything you say with skepticism." After phrasing himself in a roundabout way, Luck narrowed his eyes and let him have it. "You are a Runorata, but you didn't come as Bartolo Runorata's proxy, did you? That alone is enough to justify caution."

"What makes you think I wasn't Mr. Runorata's proxy?"

"Exposing the dealer for his important casino event to another organization? The don would never be so foolish."

"...Well said." Smiling wryly, Melvi crossed his legs, shifting his posture slightly. Even though his attitude was arrogant, his tone stayed polite. "And you're correct. I have no way to argue. It's true that I'm here of my own will, not as a member of the Runorata Family."

He confessed this easily, but it wasn't out of confusion or anxiety. "I apologize for the delayed introduction, Keith and Luck. My name is Melvi. Let me cut to the chase: Would you make a *pact* with me?"

It was as if he'd intended to disclose his intentions all along. He'd casually brought up the subject with an easy smile.

"...A pact? Not with the Runorata Family but with you as an individual?" Luck asked.

"Yes, a pact between myself and the Gandor Family."

"You don't look like you're joking. What sort of pact do you mean?"

For the first time, Melvi's expression changed. That said, only his smile dimmed slightly. "This is going very smoothly."

"Is that a problem?"

"No, no. It's just that the idea of a stripling like myself proposing a pact with a syndicate is rather ridiculous. I'd imagined you would draw your guns and rage at me for my insolence."

"Your fantasy should have continued until you were shot. Although, even that wouldn't be far enough."

"Oh? Then how far should I have let my fantasy take me?"

Luck responded to Melvi promptly, his face still blank. "Well, it's quite simple. Imagine rusty scissors, if you would."

"...Rusty scissors?"

"Now visualize the cruelest possible method of inflicting pain on a human body with those scissors, something you would never want to experience personally. I believe that would be enough," Luck said smoothly.

"So that's your angle. Here I was, ready to retort with 'Oh, is that all?' to whatever you had in mind, but I didn't think you'd tell me to picture specifics."

"Yes, I thought you'd have that sort of personality, so I was rather unkind about it. My apologies." Luck spoke in a perfunctory tone that held absolutely no remorse.

However, Melvi didn't seem particularly offended. He was still smiling. "Well now, Luck. It looks as though you and I speak the same language. That's a great help. You're not an impulsive type like that Martillo, Firo."

"Don't forget that people who see themselves in another often tend to dislike them… And? What are the details of this pact?"

"Whoops. We got sidetracked, didn't we? Beg pardon." The man was friendly to an unnatural degree; he had the air of a con artist who'd come to sell them some sketchy insurance.

The noise from Berga and Claire's fight filtered in from outside, but as they dealt with this alien factor, both Luck and Keith kept up their guards.

They'd already noticed one thing.

Melvi called himself a member of the Runoratas, but he didn't actually belong in this world.

He might be an outsider who'd stumbled into the bloody under-world, but he definitely wasn't an innocent civilian, either. As the man spoke, he seemed to be observing everything around him from a spot just outside the world itself. Luck still hadn't figured him out.

Melvi gazed into Luck's eyes from beneath his own lowered lids. "The pact is a simple one. It's a nonaggression pact."

"What do you mean?"

"I'm speaking literally. Personally, I—not the Runorata Family—am Firo Prochainezo's enemy. However, I'm not hostile toward you."

"That's—"

"I'm well aware of your ties to him, of course," Melvi interrupted. "From the way it looked last night, he seems to know my bodyguard as well." Melvi had seen through them completely.

However, Luck and the others were in regular contact with Claire, and they had no reason to shrink from his confidence.

"That makes this easy, then. Go home."

"For the sake of the Gandor Family's men, I think you should hear me out."

"If our men could get dragged into this, we wouldn't be talking with you as an individual. From that point on, the matter would be between us and the Runorata Family."

"…What I'm talking about has nothing to do with the Runora-tas, you know." Melvi stole a sidelong glance at the oldest Gandor brother, but Keith said nothing. He didn't seem inclined to make any particular contribution to the conversation.

Luck spoke for his brother as well. "Even if it's a private affair, you still belong to the Runorata Family. I don't know who you really are or what you're after, but that is fact. Your identity doesn't concern me. However, that is the world you are standing in. If you are too foolish to understand that, then talking with you any longer will be a waste of our time."

"Let me turn that around for you, Mr. Luck Gandor." Melvi narrowed his eyes slightly. "*You* are the ones who are misreading your position."

"Oh?"

"Traditions between mafia syndicates? Omertà? Revenge? Families? Worthless. I'm telling you, those limited, *human*—"

At that point, he abruptly broke off.

In the middle of his long speech, Melvi's gaze had suddenly shifted to something outside the room. Luck turned to see what he was looking at, and in that instant, Melvi launched himself off the floor. Knocking his chair over backward, moving like a carnivore going after its prey, he *sprang* up from the floor, leaping off the table and walls of the small room—and, having circled the table in the most dramatic way possible, he touched down behind Luck.

"…!" Hearing the noise, Luck began to move on reflex. Whether by coincidence or by design, Melvi had pushed the table when he'd kicked it, and it prevented Luck from standing up.

Luck's initial response had been delayed; as if mocking him, Melvi's right hand reached for his head.

In that moment, Luck turned around, and his eyes met Melvi's. The man had been hiding his true intention earlier, but there was no missing it now.

Unfortunately, there was nothing Luck could do.

⇐⇒

The past   A conversation between Czeslaw and Firo

"Say, Firo… That red-haired guy, Felix—or Claire? Is he a friend of yours?"

"Huh? Czes, have you met Claire?"

"Um, briefly."

"Hmm… He grew up in the same apartment building as me and the Gandors. He's not a bad guy… Uh, well, in terms of his work, I guess he technically is. But I'll introduce you one of these days."

"N-no, don't! Whatever you do, don't introduce us, please!"

"?"

"Never mind that. By Gandors, do you mean the Gandor Family syndicate nearby? You sure know some incredible people, Firo."

"Yeah, I guess… Actually, I'm a Martillo Family executive myself, technically. Not that I should be bragging about that to kids."

"……Yes, well, don't worry about that. Go on."

"Old Mr. Gandor took care of me, too, so of course I thought I'd join the Gandor Family. When I was making trouble in town, though, Yaguruma knocked me down, and Maiza and Ronny helped me out. When I met old Molsa, at first I was so scared I was shaking. Well, one thing led to another, and I decided to dedicate my life to the Martillo Family."

"Is that right…"

"Keith and the others were against it at first, but Claire interceded. They finally came around."

"…So he's capable of acting as a mediator."

"? Did something happen?"

"It's nothing. Or wait… When you said 'interceded,' did you mean by force?"

"Oh… Yeah, Claire's tough in a fight, but he's not the type to make us listen to him. He and Berga were constantly having fistfights, but anyway. Berga always lost those."

"I bet."

"……"

"What's wrong?"

"Czes, Claire is tough, and that's a fact. He's got better muscles and more guts than anybody around. But being a tough fighter or being good at killing doesn't mean being strong as a person."

"?"

"Claire and Berga's fights could get intense sometimes, and lots of those times they'd end up hitting Luck or me by accident."

"That must've been terrible."

"And when they were that worked up, there was just one guy who could shut them down."

"Huh?"

"Yeah. There's only one.

"He can stop Claire dead in his tracks, even if without the brawn to fight him. He's incredible."

$$\Longleftrightarrow$$

The present   The basement of Coraggioso, a jazz hall

"!" "…!"

Luck's and Melvi's eyes widened at the exact same time.

A keen-eyed man was standing between them.

"……"

Keith Gandor was as silent as ever.

What he'd done was extremely simple.

He'd grabbed Melvi's wrist as he reached for Luck's forehead, stopping him right before his fingers connected.

"Ghk…"

The pressure on his wrist erased Melvi's smile, and a little groan slipped out. Keith wasn't squeezing that hard, and on top of that, he was using his left hand. Even so, Melvi briefly feared the bones in his wrist would be crushed. He was intimidated.

Without saying a word and with no hesitation, Keith reached for Melvi's head with his right hand.

"?!"

Understanding what Keith was about to do, Melvi tried to escape by kicking him in the stomach, but the other man twisted lightly away to avoid it.

"……"

Keith still hadn't spoken, but the sharp light in his eyes showed his intentions several times more eloquently than words.

It was pure retaliation.

An eye for an eye.

A tooth for a tooth.

A blade for a blade.

A lie for a lie.

And death for death.

Finally, Melvi saw it.

Luck, the one he'd decided was the cleverest, wasn't the one he should have been the most concerned about. It was the oldest brother, the one who'd never said a word but never let his guard down.

By the time Melvi realized this, though, it was too late.

He had never felt so close to death at the hand of another. The threads of impending doom coiled around him from head to toe, fine as cobwebs and tougher than steel, and it felt as if they were trying to rip his soul apart.

That illusion swept over Melvi in less than a second.

He was about to be killed by his intended victim with comical ease, he knew, but before there was a chance of that, they were interrupted by the sound of breaking glass.

A heavy marble ashtray crashed through the window, zipping straight toward Keith's right hand.

Keith stopped reaching for Melvi's forehead and caught the ashtray instead. He was in a bizarre position: His right hand held the ashtray, and his left restrained Melvi's right wrist.

From outside the room, a laid-back voice called to him.

"Whoa, hold it—that's far enough. Okay, Keith?" Claire had

temporarily put his fight with Berga on hold and was waving at them through the broken window. "I'm technically the guy's body-guard. I'm contractually obligated to protect him so he doesn't die."

"Hey, Claire, what the hell are you lobbing ashtrays at…? Huh?"

Berga, who'd moved to grab Claire from behind, finally registered what was happening in the room.

"You slimy bastard! Whaddaya think you're doing to Keith and Luck?!"

As Berga started barreling toward the door, Claire neatly tripped him.

"Whoa?!"

Sketching a clean arc, Berga went through a half-rotation and face-planted on the floor.

"Slow your roll, fella. Keith and Luck aren't hurt. Let's hear him out first."

"Gwough… Claire, you gink!"

"Sorry, sorry. Also, it's Felix, not Claire."

Berga was writhing and holding his face. After responding to him in a laid-back way, Claire looked into the room again. "Hey, Melvi."

"What is it, Felix?"

"Well, for starters, apologize to Keith and Luck. ASAP." Claire was smiling.

"…Huh? What did you just say?" Melvi gave him a troubled smile of his own.

"I dunno what happened. The thing is, Keith's obviously out for blood, which means you did something to set him off. Keeping you alive is my job, so I'll do that. However, as their *family*, I'll also tell you this." Claire's face went completely blank. "Apologize."

"……"

For his part, Melvi had found his dauntless smile again. After a few seconds of silence, he spoke. "I'm terribly sorry about that. Even if I was only joking, I tested you, and it was very rude. Please forgive me."

He'd apologized with unexpected frankness, but both Luck and Keith knew that most of what he'd said was false.

A moment ago, he'd genuinely meant to kill them.

And because he'd revealed as much while reaching for their heads with his right hand, one of the mysteries about him had been solved.

An immortal...

Luck's eyes turned grim.

If it hadn't been for his brother, he would have been dead. He was aware of this, but as he spoke to Melvi, he didn't betray the slightest sign of agitation. "...Whether or not we forgive you, as long as Felix is protecting you, all we can do is sit here and let you walk out. Simply allowing you to escape would damage our reputation, though, so let's put it this way: It doesn't bother us. How fortunate for you."

"I'll accept your kindness and take my leave for today. My guard seems to be a double-edged sword. The wall between myself and my enemies is too thick, and I can't strike a blow, either." Lips still curved in a smile, Melvi glared coldly at Claire. Then he turned to Luck and Keith, bowed as courteously as a butler, and left the room.

The Gandor men had been watching the scene play out from a distance, and as Melvi started for the stairs that led aboveground, they moved to block his way. However, Luck made them let him through with a gesture.

"I'm looking forward to the party in February, Gandors."

With that last brief remark, still smiling, Melvi disappeared up the stairs.

"Huh? What, we're leaving already?" Claire started to follow him, then turned back to Keith and the others. "Sorry 'bout that. Guessin' that wasn't fun for you, huh. Nasty piece of work, isn't he?"

"If you're just going to apologize, don't guard him in the first place, please."

"Yeah, seriously, I'm sorry. But listen, it's for love, so tough it out for just a little."

He'd started up the stairs while he was still apologizing, but then he paused and murmured one last thing.

"See, once my contract's up, I'm taking that guy on a real thorough tour of hell."

⟺

One minute later   In the meeting room

"…So what did he come here for anyway?"

Berga had been left out of the loop, but Luck couldn't give him an answer. He knew if he told him the wrong thing, Berga just might make a beeline for the nearest place with Runorata connections and slug his way in. That's just how he was.

Melvi—that man didn't come here to talk with us. He came to massacre *us. That has to have been his goal.*

Which of them had Claire actually saved?

Had Keith genuinely intended to eat Melvi?

If Melvi really could "eat" them, then it meant *he wasn't a failed immortal like Dallas but a human who'd drunk the genuine elixir of immortality.*

His older brother was as silent as ever. His extreme reticence seemed to have grown even more pronounced in the past few years.

Either way, Luck thought there was no point in guessing at the answers. He murmured to himself, "…We may need to bolster our numbers."

That drew a reaction from Berga. "Huh? What're you talking about? I'm plenty, and you know it."

"If they hit two places, you won't be able to cover both," Luck refuted and explained what he was thinking. He spoke loudly enough that Keith could hear from a short distance away. "I know our men aren't soft, of course. I believe they're just as good as the Runorata soldiers. However, they aren't used to dealing with…aberrations like that man—people who don't use the mafia's methods. Put briefly, if two or more people like Felix show up, our fragility will be exposed."

"C'mon, like there's anybody else like Claire out there!"

"I hope you're right, but in point of fact, he's gone over to the enemy this time."

"Argh! That rat!" Berga smacked his fist into his palm.

Luck knew this was the sign that his brother had stopped thinking, so he gathered his own thoughts a bit more before continuing. "Of our executives, Nicola's the best at rough work. However, he still has some damage from the lead poisoning after he got shot up the year before last, so we can't push him too hard. Given that, the member who's most suited for this is..."

At that point, he hesitated. He really didn't want to admit who it was. Luck would have liked to end the conversation there, if at all possible.

Just then, a clear voice echoed from the stairs.

"I'm hoooome! That was an easy-peasy job, amigos! All I did was slice off two fingers, and he cried and gave back the money! What a great guy!"

Despite the frightening content of her words, the woman had a chipper tone. Luck pinched the bridge of his nose and sighed deeply.

"If she's the only option we have, that means there's something wrong with our organization."

Luck suddenly fell to thinking. Remembering the past, he muttered to himself:

"In for a penny, in for a pound... I suppose it could work..."

⟺

In an alley

"You weren't in there all that long. Did you get your business taken care of?"

"Mm-hmm. Thanks to you, Felix, it was a fool's errand."

"That's great. Wasting time is good for the soul; helps you blow off steam." Claire grinned and nodded, unfazed by Melvi's feigned gratitude.

Watching him out of the corner of his eye, Melvi thought, *Still, I didn't expect that. I thought they were oblivious about their own immortality, but...they even seemed to know about our right hands.*

The mafia are surprisingly tricky customers.

With a little sigh, he issued instructions to his bodyguard. "I'll return to the villa for today. Once we're there, you may go home as well."

"Really? If you've got time to kill, I could show you around town."

"No, that won't be necessary. Personally, I'd rather not see very much of you."

"What a coincidence. If this wasn't a job, I'd be grinding you down on a railroad track."

They both made pointed, disturbing remarks with smiles on their faces.

Without another word, they got into the car that was waiting outside.

After that car had pulled away—

Several men poked their heads out of an alley.

"That's the Gandor Family's office, for sure?"

"Yes. We ID'd it earlier, the time they went to the mattresses with Gustavo."

"…They're even letting that new punk handle negotiations with other families?"

"Nah, he's just a dealer. I can't see him having that much authority…"

Even as the man spoke, another guy's hand closed around his throat.

"Gack… Gwah…!"

"'*Just*' a dealer? Did you just call Miz Carlotta's job 'just'? Huh? Can you do it? Can you swindle one red cent out of a casino pigeon? Huh?"

"Ghk… S-sorry…" Tears filled the coworker's eyes.

Shoving him away, the man snarled, "That prick waltzed in and stole Miz Carlotta's chance to shine as a dealer right out from under her! That fishy greenhorn can't keep doing whatever the hell he wants!"

"But listen… The boss made that call," a third man reminded him.

The guy got himself under control. "…Yeah, that's right. That's why we've been keeping an eye on him, waiting for him to slip up. Although, I never thought he'd show his true colors this fast."

"Are we gonna report him to the boss?"

"Nah, we'll make him *disappear*. On a riverbed, say, or into some dog's belly." He wore a menacing smile, as hateful as his remark. "If we wait until people start making noise about it, then say we saw him visit the Gandors' office, we can make it look like he was their spy."

Then he made one more foolishly fearless and woefully uninformed remark.

"Then we can just pin all the blame on that ginger bodyguard of his."

⟺

In the car

Unaware that this dangerous conversation was occurring after he'd left, Melvi was thinking something even more dangerous than the men who'd been shadowing him.

So I couldn't get the Gandors. Well, what's done is done. I'll wait until the day of the casino opening…then kill them off slowly.

He turned his face toward the window, closing his eyes, so the bodyguard who sat next to him couldn't read his expression. Behind his eyelids, he pictured the young guy he'd met the previous day.

Firo Prochainezo, huh? He didn't look like a big deal. He sneered, and then hatred welled up inside him. *So that two-bit loser got Szilard's memories? He has* those *memories, and he's still letting himself rot away in a dinky mafia casino?*

Ironically, the reason behind his hate was the same as that of the Runorata men who were watching him.

There wouldn't be much fun in simply "eating" him. Until the day of the casino event, I'll consume everything from his world bit by bit. Then when I'm done, I'll experience his agonies vicariously—as my own memories...

As he indulged in this bizarre fantasy, he smiled out the window.

That should be its own kind of fun.

Unlike his well-practiced smile, this one was genuine.

All right...I wonder how many of his acquaintances will disappear today.

Chapter 13　　Violence Creates Nothing

It had been more than two hundred years since Maiza Avaro lost his younger brother, consumed by Szilard Quates's hand.

The brothers had been born and raised in Lotto Valentino, a port town in southern Italy. Both the town and their father had been trammeled by aristocratic conventions, and Gretto was the one who'd most wanted to escape them. However, before they reached the New World, he'd lost everything.

Meanwhile, after his brother had been stolen from him, Maiza had come up against the stark fact that no matter how many decades or centuries he spent on regret, there were some things he could never recover. He'd been forced to see, in the worst possible way, that immortals weren't all-powerful.

Even now, he could remember his brother's face clearly.

At the very least, those who'd survived had to keep their memories of his brother forever—that was why he would never forget his brother's face.

Or so he'd thought until half a day ago, when he'd encountered that young man in the casino run by his subordinate.

That was definitely Gretto's face…

The more he recalled it, the more his memories distorted Gretto's real face. Now he couldn't remember the differences between it and the fellow he'd met the previous day.

It was as if that man's face was overwriting his brother's features, and Maiza was racked with guilt.

His brother had been killed in a time before photographs, so his face remained only in the memories of the immortals who'd known him. He wished they'd at least had a family portrait painted—but no amount of regret would make that nonexistent portrait a reality.

If a skilled artist from the group on the ship is still alive... Victor said he had confidence in his memory, but...

Even as he wondered whether his old friend had the skill to draw a portrait based on memory alone, Maiza was eating his breakfast, just as he always did.

Maiza's apartment was on the outskirts of Little Italy. The neighborhood had always been a poor one, home to many immigrants with few resources, but his building had been built before the Depression and was relatively new.

Maiza had enough money to buy a house on the edge of Manhattan, but since he lived alone and didn't see the need to take up that much space, he'd continued to shuttle between a handful of apartments.

It had begun as a habit he'd developed while hiding from Szilard Quates, living in places where he would blend in. Szilard, his greatest threat, had died in the fall of 1930, but Maiza still hadn't moved in the five years since. After that, he hadn't needed to hide. That said, he'd gotten used to living this way, and he had no desire for a big house. Living somewhere pointlessly spacious would have reminded him of their aristocratic mansion in his hometown.

What happened to that house after I fled the town in 1711? he thought out of nowhere. He couldn't claim to have no memories there, but the only things it reminded him of were things he'd rather forget.

His father had been possessed by a lust for aristocratic power and been the cause of many of the town's tragedies. However, the fact that those events had occurred was what had made it possible for him to be here, more than two hundred years later, eating breakfast in a foreign land.

I never thought I'd end up remembering them like this.

He ate a few scraps of cheese for dessert, then slowly got to his feet and went to brush his teeth.

As he went, he was turning his own past over in his mind.

Afterward, he got ready in the usual way. He pulled on his coat, preparing to head for the Martillo Family office—and by then, his mind had already switched over to that of the *contaiuolo*, the family's treasurer.

All right. First, how are we going to compensate for the damages to the casino?

After making himself presentable like always, he opened the door as he did on every other day.

A tailor said he'd made some counterfeit brand-name bags and asked us to buy them, but even if we sold them off cheaply, there's no telling how many we'd move in a recession like this one...

Just like always, he kept running calculations in his head.

Even after the disturbance at the casino the night before, and even though the city had just been thrown into an uproar by the mysterious air raid, his steps as he made for the office were as regular as ever.

After all, he was an executive. If he let himself feel disturbed, it would affect the entire organization, and that wouldn't do. He understood this, so he made sure to act calm and collected.

He went down the hall in the usual way, descended the stairs normally. There was one thing out of place, though.

As he walked downstairs from his room on the third floor, just as he passed the second-floor landing...

...a figure appeared from the hallway and brought a metal pipe down on the back of his head.

⇔

At Fred's clinic

"Say, Isaac?" said a woman in an old-fashioned nurse uniform.

"What is it, Miria?" Isaac Dian responded. He was wearing a white lab coat, but he really didn't look like a doctor.

"Why are we dressed like doctors?"

"Well, because we're assisting one. We have to look the part."

This seemed to stir up more doubts in Miria Harvent. "But we can't heal anything, you know?"

At that, Isaac puffed out his chest confidently. "It's fine, Miria! I've caught colds before, but after I got some good, solid sleep, they cleared right up!"

"Oh! Me too! I got a bump once, but I put ice on it, and it got better!"

"There, you see?! We can heal ourselves, so you could say we're terrific doctors!"

"You're right! That's amazing!"

Isaac and Miria were the same as ever. However, the man who was standing behind them looked rather harried. "I think you two should probably get your heads examined."

"Huh?! Really?! But mine doesn't hurt."

"Yes, mine's fine, too."

They hadn't picked up on the sarcasm and only blinked in confusion.

"Still, if you're worried about us, you must be a real swell guy!"

"Yes, Nightingale! Hippocrates! Hideyo Noguchi!"

They'd begun thanking him instead, which only made him feel guilty.

"Huh? No, uh… Sorry," he apologized on reflex.

"Why are you apologizing, Who?"

"Yes, why?"

"Nah… Just forget it."

Sighing, the man they'd called Who went back to his work, thinking, *We sure got some weird ones this time. They started wearing old uniforms all of a sudden. It's weird that Mr. Fred let 'em do that. They don't seem like bad people, though.*

The three of them were in a clinic run by a doctor named Fred.

In addition to the clinic, Fred operated a welfare lodging house. The lodging house was short-staffed, so he'd asked his supporters if they could recommend any reliable assistants, and a restaurant proprietor named Molsa Martillo had sent this couple over.

"Well, well. If I recall, you two were..."
"Aaaah! It's the magician from the train!"
"Yes, the gray one!"
"I see... This must be fate. If Mr. Martillo has recommended you, then I really mustn't turn you away."

Following that conversation, Fred had hired them on the spot.

The majority of the cargo that went to the lodging house was food, and due to the recession, workers occasionally just made off with it. As a result, the job required people whose backgrounds had been checked pretty carefully.

Well, they don't look like the type who'd snatch groceries, Who, Fred's assistant, thought.

He didn't have an inkling that Isaac and Miria were burglars who'd had a very small part of America in an uproar until just a few years ago. He'd assumed they were good people who could teach the average child a thing or two about innocence.

"The doc's going to take you over to the lodging house in just a little while. Until then, help me load up this cargo. While you're out, Lebreau and I will hold the fort."

Lebreau—just as he'd mentioned that name, the clinic's front door opened and the man himself poked his head in. "Well, well. Dr. Fred isn't here yet?"

"Hey, Lebreau. You showed up, huh?"

"Oh! Mr. Lebreau, was it?! We haven't seen you in hours!"

"Yes, what a pleasant reunion!"

Lebreau Fermet Viralesque turned a brisk smile on the people who'd greeted him. "Good morning. Isaac and Miria, starting today, I look forward to working with you."

He'd gotten to know Fred the other day, and since he had medical knowledge, he came to help out at the clinic from time to time as his assistant, like Who.

Who had begun as an amateur and learned on the job. Conversely, this man had had a vast amount of medical knowledge to begin with. He was also skilled with a scalpel, which made him very useful during surgeries.

"Well, now we just have to wait for the doc."

Who had just finished packing groceries for the lodging house kitchen into boxes when a shadow fell across the clinic's entrance.

The door glass had gone dark, so he assumed Fred had shown up, but the shadow was too big. A car had stopped in front of the entrance.

"Oh, come on. They can't park there. They'll block the door," Who said with a scowl.

The clinic entrance was a simple gate, and the car was right up against its pillars. Visitors wouldn't be able to get in without climbing through the vehicle or going over it.

"I'll go ask them to move," Lebreau said, already walking toward the entrance, but as soon as he opened the door, a man appeared out of nowhere and slugged him in the stomach.

"Ghk...?!"

Lebreau bent double, and the intruder kicked him over.

Then four men got out of the car and piled into the clinic. Including the first man, that made five. At first glance, they didn't look unusual, but there was a unique hard edge to them that made Who guess they had underworld connections.

"Wh-who are you fellas?!" Who ran over to the floundering Lebreau, trying to help him up.

The men completely ignored his question and asked one of their own instead. "There's only one jane, so Miria is obvious. Which one's Isaac?"

"Huh? Me? N-never mind that. What do you think you're doing to Lebreau?!" Isaac said, pointing to himself on reflex. Despite hearing his name so suddenly, he was more concerned about the sudden violence.

"We're against violence!" Miria protested.

The men exchanged glances and started whispering among themselves.

("...Looks like that's him.")

("It don't matter. We're snatching everybody here anyway.")

("All of 'em?")

("Yeah, they said it'd work better if we pulled in a few people who had nothing to do with this.")

They were conversing quietly, but they were so close that Who heard them loud and clear. He felt a chill run down his spine.

Hey, whoa, no, c'mon! What the hell is this?! What did I just get dragged into?!

That bus... Did they block the gate so we couldn't make a break for it?! Did Isaac and Miria pull something sketchy?!

Several questions surfaced in his head, but Isaac and Miria didn't seem to know anything about this, either. They were wary of the intruders, but they went on kicking up a fuss.

"Wh-what are you people?! Kidnappers?!"

"Yes, the kidnapping industry! 'Ndrangheta!"

"Too bad for you, though! Right now, we don't have a dime!"

"You'll end up working for free!"

The thugs didn't respond. Impassively getting down to business, they reached into their jackets and took out leather bags packed with sand: blunt weapons commonly referred to as blackjacks or saps. They were obviously planning to knock out the entire group. One of the men hefted up his sap for a swing at Who's temple.

"Wh-whoa, hold up a minute! Okay, okay! We'll go with you quietly! Just don't hurt us, all right?! Please?!" Who begged, sitting flat on the ground, but his plea fell unheard.

Silently, they raised their weapons.

Without a scrap of mercy or hesitation, they brought them down hard.

Who, Isaac, and Miria, and even the men—none of them noticed Lebreau curled up, hugging his stomach with his face turned away to hide his gloating smile.

⟺

Meanwhile　　The restaurant and bar Alveare

"Huh? The place seems kinda empty today."

After ordering his men to clean up the casino, Firo had stopped by the restaurant to make a report to Molsa and Maiza. However, things were quieter than he would have expected.

Ronny had said he'd tell Molsa about the previous day's incident, so Firo had thought Molsa might have some new orders for him today. He'd been a little nervous, and the uncommonly quiet restaurant was making his nerves worse.

"Oh, Firo. Annie hasn't come in yet, either."

"Huh, that's unusual."

As far as Firo knew, Annie had never been late or skipped work before.

Seina, the proprietress, seemed worried that she'd taken ill. Firo knew what Annie really was, though, and he was worried about something else.

Did she get some sort of Huey-related job?

Hilton was a group of women who all shared a mind with one of Huey's daughters, Leeza Laforet. Their knowledge and wills had been completely absorbed into her, and their individual minds no longer existed.

Annie was one of those women. If she'd deviated from her normal routine, he had to guess it was because she was performing some sort of task on Huey's orders.

It might have something to do with yesterday.

He did think that making connections willy-nilly might not be wise, but after all, the trouble with Melvi involved immortals. It wouldn't be odd if they were connected somewhere.

Firo felt strangely uneasy, but for the moment, he sat down and waited for Maiza and Molsa to come in.

About five minutes later, the door opened. The newcomer was Kanshichirou Yaguruma, a high-level executive.

"Yaguruma, good morning!"

"Hey, Firo. Glad to see you're looking well. You didn't run into any trouble?"

"?" Perplexed, Firo hadn't expected that from Yaguruma. "Trouble...? What do you mean?"

"Well, maybe it's this lousy economy. The public seems to be on edge after that business with the airplanes yesterday. Some folks were saying, 'We're at war now' and 'It's the end of the world.' I even heard some women gossiping that Martians had attacked."

"Oh..." Firo felt vaguely that the incident with the airplanes was linked to the immortals as well, so his feelings about this were complicated.

"I got jumped by some of those twitchy folks on my way here."

"?!"

"Oh, they came at me from behind, swinging some weapon around. They probably thought they'd caught me by surprise, but I grabbed the fellow's arm and threw him. The others got spooked and took to their heels."

Yaguruma laughed, but to Firo, it was no laughing matter.

Right on the heels of the previous day, his superior had been attacked.

He hadn't been naïve enough to think the enemy wouldn't try anything until the day the Runoratas' casino opened. Under these circumstances, he had to suspect there was a connection.

His premonition proved to be correct in the worst possible way.

The door opened again, and in walked several men who obviously weren't on the right side of the law. That said, they also didn't seem affiliated with the Martillos.

They all went up to Seina, who ran the restaurant. The first words out of their leader's mouth were, "Say, is there a fella named Firo Prochainezo here?"

"What's with you boys? What brought this on?" Seina raised an eyebrow.

The man sat down at the counter in an overly familiar way and went on asking questions. "We know this is where the Martillos hang out. If you hide him, you're gonna regret it."

"Hey, you need me for something?" Firo called from the end of the counter.

The new visitors glanced at one another before striding over to him.

"So you're Firo, huh? You look like your photo... Now that I've got you in the flesh, you really are just like he said."

"...You wanna tell me what you heard and the name of the guy who told you?"

"Agent Noah told us you had a girly little punk face."

Firo scowled for two different reasons. *Edward. That lousy bastard. So that means...these guys are from the BOI?*

Edward Noah was on the side of the law, and Firo had never liked him. In any case, messing with him would cause trouble for the family, so Firo did his best to just steer clear whenever he could. Unfortunately, they tended to run into each other whenever there was an incident. The ties that bound them were the sort that both would have loved to shake off, but neither could.

"Well, you tell that bastard something from me. Tell him, 'You be careful you don't get your face beaten in one day. It'd be a real shame if nobody could tell if you were a woman yourself afterward.'"

He'd meant for the line to be witheringly sarcastic. However, the Bureau men exchanged glances.

"...Your warning's a little late."

"Huh?"

"This morning, Agent Noah got jumped and hurt *bad* by some thugs."

"...He what?" This was a bolt from the blue. Firo's eyes went wide, and he hauled the nearest man up by his shirtfront. "Hey, what's this about?"

"According to the drifter who saw it happen, they jumped him this morning when he left his apartment building. Agent Noah was on the ground, and several men were whaling on him."

"Sure, the guy's an asshole, but... Did somebody have it in for him?"

"...If I were you, I wouldn't be playing innocent." The man glared at him.

Firo drew his eyebrows together. "What?"

"There was a hat the same color as yours at the scene."

"What?! Hey, you're not telling me you suspect me, right? Over that?!" Firo yelled, irritated and anxious that he might have stumbled into a trap—but the agent shook his head.

"No, we don't think you're the perp. Victor said so, too."

"?"

"The hat had 'You're next' written on it, and it had been *cut in half.* We think it was a message for you."

Firo frowned, confused. "Hey... Whoa, wait! That can't be right! A message for me...? It's not even like Edward's my pal; we're enemies! Why'd they jump him?!"

"That's what we'd like to know," the agent told him. There was hatred for both Firo and the culprits in his eyes. "All we do know is that Agent Noah got dragged into your mess, scumbag. I've got absolutely no idea why they chose him when he's your enemy."

Their message delivered, the agents turned away from him. "Listen up, Firo Prochainezo. If you figure anything out, let us know ASAP. Don't forget that, as far as the assistant director's concerned, you're just a pawn."

"Maybe so, but remember I'm not *your* pawn."

"...In that case, make sure you keep your head down." After muttering one last comment, the agents left the restaurant. "Unless you'd like to take another naked stroll down Broadway over in Alcatraz?"

Even after they were gone, Firo kept glaring at the entrance.

"Good grief. If it was the same crew that attacked me. I should have nabbed at least one of 'em," Yaguruma remarked.

Switching gears, Firo turned to Seina and asked in a serious tone, "Where's Mr. Molsa today? ...And Maiza?"

"...Now that you mention it, Maiza's not here yet," Seina said.

"Mr. Molsa came in, same as always; he's in the back now. I think Ronny's shuffling papers at the office."

Firo was relieved their boss was safe, but the fact that Maiza wasn't there made his expression cloud over. "I'll go check up on him."

Yaguruma spoke up, admonishing him. "Firo, wait. What good will it do if you wander around out there yourself?"

"But I'm nervous…"

"You should go check on Annie first, then. Don't worry about Maiza."

"Huh? But why…?"

True, if Edward had been attacked because of his connection with him, then he should've been worrying about Annie, Isaac, and Miria, too. And yet, when he thought about what had happened the previous day—the man who'd been a dead ringer for Maiza's kid brother—it made him fear that Maiza was the one most likely to get pulled into this mess.

Firo couldn't keep his anxiety hidden, and Yaguruma tried to calm him down. "It's fine, Firo. Yes, Maiza's the *contaiuolo*, which means all he does is count money. On top of that, your knife skills are better than his now.

"But in combat, Maiza's several times stronger than you. I guarantee it."

⇔

Little Italy   The stairs of Maiza's apartment building

"Wha…?"

The startled cry came from the man who'd tried to bring the iron pipe down on Maiza's back. He'd swung the weapon with all his might, but his target had simply vanished.

Of course, it wasn't as if Maiza had evaporated like mist. Maiza had simply slipped into his blind spot.

"Beg pardon."

Just as the assailant thought he'd heard his target's voice from somewhere on his right, pain ran through his chin.

"Gwuh...!" he sputtered, swearing he saw a thick square bar of lumber being shoved straight through his face from one side to the other. For a moment, a visual of his torn-off jaw sailing away flashed through his mind, and then pain raced down his spinal cord—and before it even reached his fingertips, his rattled brain shut down.

As a matter of fact, his jaw had been dislocated, but it hadn't been torn off or flung across the hall, and he hadn't been stabbed by anything. It was the overwhelming impact of the high-speed palm strike that had put the image in his head.

The man crumpled from the knees, like a marionette with cut strings.

Without sparing him a glance, Maiza walked into the second-floor hallway. His steps were calm and measured.

The two men who were waiting there glared back at him, startled and wide-eyed. They hadn't expected him to emerge completely unscathed.

Are they amateurs? Maiza wondered, noticing they hadn't planned for unexpected contingencies. Regardless, carelessness led to mistakes. He wasn't overconfident enough to assume his own victory.

As Maiza tried to puzzle out who his opponents were, one of the men took a roscoe from his jacket.

"...Don't move."

Obediently, Maiza stopped in his tracks and slowly raised his hands. "Calm yourselves, please. I'm unarmed, and I don't intend to resist."

"......"

"Didn't the first fellow attack me with a blunt instrument because gunshots would attract attention you couldn't afford? Since we have the chance, let's resolve this peacefully," Maiza proposed.

The remaining men turned to each other. After a short pause, the man with the gun tightened his grip on it. "Face the other way, then lie down on the floor."

"All right." Slowly, Maiza turned his back to the men and got on his knees.

The attackers exchanged nods. Then, as Maiza set his hands on the floor, the man without a gun walked over to him, took out a black-jack weapon from his jacket, and raised it high. He took another step forward in the narrow hall.

The gunman realized they'd made an awful blunder. Now that the second man had stepped forward, he was blocking his line of fire. His partner was inadvertently obscuring their target, and he had a really nasty feeling about what was going to happen. Although he understood that, he didn't know what he should do, and that hesitation blunted his thoughts at a crucial time.

"Gah…!"

By the time he heard his companion scream, it was too late. A sharp pain ran through his right hand. He looked over to see something shocking…

His trigger finger was lying on the hallway floor like a discarded cigar butt.

A few seconds earlier, as Maiza had lowered himself to the ground, he'd propelled himself back to his feet using only the muscles in his arms and kicked the closest man in the stomach. Using his groaning enemy's body as a shield, he'd pushed him forward. At the same time, he'd drawn his knife, then reached out from behind his human shield and severed the finger of the man with the gun.

"Ghk…!"

When Maiza watched the finger fall and heard the resulting scream from the gunman, the *contaiuolo* struck again. He slashed at the man's hand a second time with his bloody knife, making him drop the gun.

"GwaaAAAAaaah?!"

Once Maiza confirmed the gun wasn't in his opponent's hand anymore, he caught the ear of his shield and yanked it to the side.

"Eep?!"

With an ugly crunching noise, the ear began to tear away from the man's face.

As if his instinct compelled him not to let his ear be severed, the man's whole body toppled over in that direction. Maiza swept his feet out from under him, sending him to the floor, then promptly stepped on his throat.

"…! ……?!?! ——!"

Maiza heard the crushing of the man's Adam's apple and blood bubble between his lips as he writhed on the floor.

Without thinking, the remaining attacker bent over, trying to retrieve his gun with his left hand. Maiza promptly sent his knee squarely in the man's face.

"Bwugk!" he cried as his back arched. Blood spurted from his broken nose.

However, Maiza didn't ease up; he kicked the man into the wall, back first. The impact knocked all the air out of his lungs.

"Gah…!" The man gave a bloody groan, and the next thing he knew, the blade of a knife was resting against his chin.

"All right. Let's have a peaceful little chat," Maiza said.

Two men lay unconscious, their eyes rolled back, one on the landing and the other in the hall. The remaining man was bleeding heavily from his mouth and nose, with a knife pressed to his throat.

Then there was the finger that lay at Maiza's feet.

Peaceful, indeed. What struck the attacker as scarier than anything was the serenity in Maiza's voice after all that bloodshed. Even the smile on his face was the wry sort a parent might wear when watching their mischievous child. His sharp eyes were watching calmly.

The assailant thought back on when they had held Maiza at gunpoint and then when Maiza had cut off his finger. He might have had that same expression then.

Through his pain, the man felt a chill work its way down his spine.

"Now, then. Why did you three attack…?" Maiza began. "No, that's too roundabout, isn't it?"

"…?"

How was getting the answer to a direct question *roundabout*? That was concerning, but fear had paralyzed him, and he couldn't give too much thought to what it meant.

"Which side do you belong to?" Maiza asked.

"...???"

"By 'which,' I mean, did you attack me because of my connections to the immortals, or was it for something else?"

"......—!"

At that, the man's face changed color slightly. However, he still didn't speak. He trembled, and his eyes darted around, unsure of where to look.

"Answers don't come more foolish than silence, you know. If you stay silent and hostile, I'll have to conclude..." Maiza's placid expression was at odds with his behavior. With the knife still held against one of the man's vital spots, he bent down and dexterously retrieved the index finger from the hall floor. "...that you are picking a fight, not with me as an individual but with the Martillo Family."

Maiza locked eyes with him, and in that instant, an even more powerful chill struck the attacker's spine: The face of the man who was torturing him was perfectly still.

It wasn't twisted with hatred or dominated by sadistic desires. Only an endlessly deep, cold emotion seeped out of his half-open eyes.

"......" The man's lips and knees trembled, but even then, he didn't identify himself.

Maiza tossed the severed finger toward him. There was a flash of light, and the knife pinned the finger to the wall next to the man's face.

Now cut in two, the finger fell, but Maiza caught the pieces in his free hand before they hit the floor. This would have been a perfect opportunity for the attacker to make a run for it, but because of the blow to his back, his body wasn't responsive enough.

Maiza held the two pieces in front of the man's eyes and spoke, his expression unchanged: "I'm going to shove this finger in deep enough that they won't be able to extract it without surgery. Which would you prefer: your *nose* or your *ear*?"

"H-huh?" The attacker didn't understand. The bleeding from his nose hadn't stopped.

Maiza went on impassively. "If you can't choose, let's make it your eyes." He brushed the man's eyelashes with the severed finger.

"WaaaAAAaaaaAAAh! Aaagh, no! I dunnoooooo! I just—! I'm just following orders…!" the man screamed, shaking his head from side to side like a spring-loaded doll.

"From whom?" Maiza asked calmly.

The man's mouth flapped futilely as he tried to give some sort of answer. "Wha—…? Duh…duh-d-d— D-d-d-d-d-d-duh-d— L-lo-ra— Ra-ruh-ruh— AaaaAauAAaah…" His eyes rolled back in his head, and he passed out.

"Drat. I must have frightened him too much," Maiza muttered. Then he heaved a sigh. "I just can't seem to do it the way the Gandors' Tick does…"

With no other options, Maiza decided to wait until they woke up. However, he was traveling on foot, and he really couldn't walk through town carrying an unconscious man.

I'll put one in my room for now, then.

As he was pondering which of the unconscious men seemed likely to know the most about the situation, he heard a soft *clack* from a corner of the hall.

"?"

When he turned around, a small tube was lying near the border of the hall and the landing, emitting billows of thick smoke.

"What's that?!"

Maiza leaped back, guessing that it might explode. However, instead of an explosion, it spit out an even larger cloud of smoke. On top of that, multiple sets of footsteps echoed from the stairs.

"!"

Reinforcements, hmm?

If they were planning to charge into this smoke, should he assume they had a way to move even when visibility was bad? He was wary of this, and he also considered the possibility the smoke was poisonous gas. He backed away, keeping out of the smoke screen, and hid around a corner of the hall.

In the end, nobody struck at him from inside the cloud.

And when the smoke cleared several minutes later, there was

nothing in the hall but bloodstains and the pieces of finger. The voices of rubberneckers echoed up from the floor below.

Maiza had thought those footsteps had belonged to reinforcements, but they hadn't been coming to attack him. They'd only retrieved their unconscious comrades.

Realizing this, he sighed heavily. He was frustrated with himself for not taking one of them outside the smoke screen with him when he retreated.

"I really can't talk like an expert in front of Firo, can I...?"

$$\Longleftrightarrow$$

Fred's clinic

"Hiyaaaaah!"

Just before the sap connected with Who's back, Isaac threw himself between them.

He'd probably been planning to shield Who and Lebreau by catching the blow on his own back, but he was a moment too late, and the hard leather weapon walloped his wrist.

"Yagh?!"

His momentum pitched him to the floor, and he rolled around, shrieking.

"Waaaaargh?! What the...? Ow! Ow! Seriously, that hurt! What the heck is that thing?!"

Isaac flopped around, cradling his stinging, numbed right hand, and Miria screamed.

"Aaaaaaah, Isaaaaaac!"

However, the attackers' reaction to that fragile shriek was merciless. "It'll be bad news if they hear her outside. Get the doll first."

"Right." Without hesitating, another man took the same type of weapon his companion had used out of his jacket and started toward Miria.

"H-hey! Even if you're the only one who makes it, get out of here!

Run!" Who yelled in a hurry. No matter how he thought about it, though, she wouldn't be able to escape. Even if Miria knew where the back door was, they'd probably catch her before she got to it. Maybe he could keep their enemies pinned down while she ran outside and called for help; Who scrambled to his feet.

Another man loomed behind him with a bludgeon.

As the back of Who's head was about to take a vicious blow—

—the shrill sound of a collision pierced their eardrums.

It was nothing like the noise of leather striking flesh. It was the sharp screech of metal against metal.

"?!"

Nobody in the room could figure out what was making that noise, but it seemed to be coming from outside the clinic, directly in front of the main door.

The noise didn't stop after just one time. It rang out at regular intervals—for a second time, then a third—and the intervals between the sounds gradually grew shorter.

"What's that…?"

The attacker who was closest to the door opened it suspiciously, and saw a man in blue coveralls swinging around a giant wrench and wrecking the car they'd used to hide the entrance. The heap had already been partially dismantled, and components littered the road.

"Wha…?! H-hey, you! What the hell?!"

This was weirder than anything the men could have imagined; they were suddenly much less confident, and a lot more pissed off. But even when they started yelling, the man in the coveralls didn't apologize or shrink back in fear.

"Let me tell you a real sad, sad story…," the man in the coveralls said, twirling his wrench.

"Huh…?"

"My man Ladd is eating breakfast in that restaurant over there. He told me, 'Go see if the clinic's open yet,' so I had my orders, but my way was blocked by a fateful ordeal… There was a car parked right in front of the clinic, and I couldn't see what was going on inside."

Smacking the wrench into his left palm, the man in the coveralls kept going.

"But, see, if I'd climbed over some total stranger's car with my muddy boots, it wouldn't just be on me; they'd think Ladd and my pals had no class, either... I wasn't strong enough to pick up the car and carry it, though, and I didn't have the key to move it. Oh, what could I do to overcome this ordeal imposed on me by God?! What lay beyond this trial?! That's right, the clinic!"

The man kept on shouting incomprehensibly, and the attackers shared frowns with one another.

One person understood, though. When Who heard the newcomer's voice and unique phrasing, his eyes widened. "Uh... I'm pretty sure that's...Ladd's underling... Is that Graham?"

And actually, did he say something about Ladd just now?

As Who watched him dubiously, Graham Specter looked up at the building and, with a sudden burst of energy, pointed his wrench sharply at the clinic entrance. "Yes, it's the clinic! Say a guy who's gonna save the world someday has a heart attack, and he can't get in because this boiler is in the way! This bus is a threat to all humanity and life! What do I have to do to save the world? If I get this heap out of the way, the world will be saved! In other words! I'm the one who's going to save the world! And right now, I can't get into the clinic! That proves that this car is indeed the enemy of the world!"

Continuing his gibberish, Graham hooked the enormous wrench onto the front of the car and skillfully removed the bumper.

"Fun... Let me tell you a fun story! If I'm the savior of the world, and this car is the world's enemy, then I can do whatever I want to it without repercussions!"

Oh yeah, now I remember. This guy is an idiot, Who thought, quirking an eyebrow. He took the chance to help Lebreau up and move him to a corner of the room, away from the attackers.

Meanwhile, Graham went on with his huge, self-contained argument.

"In that case, this is easy. If I can't pick the bus up, I can just break it down into its component parts and carry those! Then, if I put them together again over there, the car will be saved, too... True, this heap is the enemy of the world, but it's also part of the world. Thus, as the world's savior, I decided I should save its enemy, the car, as well. Is that clear?!"

He threw his wrench into the air for no reason, then caught it with a *thwap*, pointing it at the attackers.

The situation was far too surreal, and the men were confused for a little while, but Isaac and Miria broke the stunned silence.

"This is big, Miria! Apparently, that guy is the savior of the world!"

"Do you think he'll save us, too?!"

"Let's hope we're part of the world!"

"What if he thinks we're Martians...?"

When the attackers heard Isaac's and Miria's enthusiasm from behind them, they came to their senses. Isaac had apparently recovered from the pain in his hand, and he hugged Miria close to protect her from them.

The group's leader screamed at his men, his face beet red. "Somebody go shut up that imbecile in front of the car! We're drawing a crowd!"

Thanks to the air raid the previous evening, there were already more police on the streets than usual. If the noise didn't quieten down soon, it wouldn't be long before the cops came running.

After he'd watched two of his men climb over the car and head for the man with the wrench, the attacker said, "We'll ditch the bus. Scram out the back door or a window; we'll just take Isaac and Miria and run." Then he glared at Who and Lebreau. "Lousy luck, fellas. We're getting rid of you two here."

"What the hell?! That ain't right!" Who protested.

The leader ignored him, taking a knife out of his jacket.

However, the advantage he'd won through violence ended right there.

It was wiped out by another, even more unfair form of violence that appeared out of nowhere.

As the knife wielder walked toward Who, a loud crash and screams rang out behind him. Once he realized the screams belonged to his goons, he whipped around.

One of the men had somehow been hoisted up on top of the car. He'd collapsed, and his limbs were bent in all the wrong directions.

The other lay beside the vehicle, with a sizable dent in the neighborhood of his nose and front teeth.

"Theeere we go!"

One of the car's remaining doors came off with a sharp *crunch*, and a man climbed through the half-demolished vehicle, stepping inside the gate. He cracked his neck, then turned his eyes to the scene inside the clinic.

He saw three remaining assailants—one of whom was holding somebody familiar at knifepoint.

"Heya, Who. You busy?" he called.

When Who heard that voice, his eyes went from the knife to the door. As he registered the man who stood there, his expression shifted into a complicated mix of 50 percent shock, 40 percent worry, and 10 percent relief.

"L...Ladd! If it ain't Ladd!"

"Looks like you're still getting dragged into trouble, huh."

"Wha—?! What are you doing here...?"

"Well, your 'Closed' sign was out yesterday, so I sent Graham over to take a look-see, and then I heard bangs and clangs all the way over at the restaurant where I was. That's the sound he makes when he wrecks cars, so I figured there was a party goin' on and came running over. And I was right." Ladd shrugged.

Who thought, *What the heck is he doing in New York?! Where's he been all this time?!* and sundry other things, but then he remembered the knife was still right in front of him. He backed away slowly so as not to provoke the guy who held it.

"What's with you? You wanna die, pal?" said the man with the knife, but cold sweat had broken out on his face.

Ignoring him, Ladd took a closer look around the room. Then he saw somebody unexpected, and his eyes went wide. "Huh...? Hmm? Hey. Isaac? Don't tell me that's Isaac?"

"Huh? …Aah! Ladd! It's Ladd!"

Seeing that they were both startled, Who muttered, "What, you know each other?"

Ladd chuckled at the quiet comment. He didn't seem to care about the guy with the knife anymore as he filled Who in.

"Well, we did a little time together at Alcatraz."

"A…Alcatraz?" Who asked, surprised.

What's he talking about? Alcatraz? As in the prison? Ladd's one thing, but there's no way Isaac was in a place like that.

Who decided it was either a mistake or some sort of code word. However, he wasn't bold enough to pursue the question with a knife right in front of him.

Meanwhile, the goon holding that knife had gotten scared. *Did he say Alcatraz?* he thought.

Of his two companions who were on the ground outside, this guy had apparently taken out one of them. He could tell that much, but he didn't know who the guy was, apart from the fact that he was obviously dangerous.

If that guy had spent time in Alcatraz, there was a good possibility he was a criminal—and highly dangerous. Maybe he belonged to a big-time mafia syndicate. If that was the case, tangling with him wouldn't bring about anything good.

On that thought, the guy slipped the knife back into his coat and slowly put some space between himself and the other people around him.

"Huh? What gives, fella? You're at a party, and you're putting your piece away?" Ladd complained, still smiling.

In contrast, Who breathed a sigh of relief. "I—I'm glad you changed your mind. I dunno what you're after, but let's talk it out first, all right?"

However, the attackers ignored Who. Instead, they exchanged wordless glances, signaling one another.

Ladd didn't like this. He stepped in, preparing to take out the remaining three, but then the man who'd stowed away his knife took out a grenade-like object from his jacket instead.

He pulled the pin and dropped it on the floor.

A smoke screen billowed out of it with abnormal force, and white darkness filled the clinic almost all the way to the gate.

When the smoke cleared, the attackers had vanished. Even the two Graham and Ladd had KO'd were gone.

"Huh. Damn. They ran off." Ladd didn't sound particularly surprised or frustrated by this. He glanced around. "Well, they looked boring anyway."

"A-are we…saved?" Who timidly scanned the area, but his head was still all muddled. "Hey, Ladd, what are you doing in town?"

But Ladd was too busy talking to Isaac. "Hey there! It's been forever and a half, huh, Isaac! I knew you and Firo were pals, but who'd have figured I'd run into you when I came looking for Who!"

"Oh, we just met Who yesterday ourselves."

"Say, Isaac? Is this man your friend?" Who asked, trying to cut in.

Ladd ignored him. "Oh, is this sweet little lady your girl Miria?"

They were having a nice, friendly chat, and Who couldn't get a word in. From behind, Lebreau set a hand on his shoulder.

"They seem to know each other. We shouldn't disturb them. I'll go check the back door and the patients in the clinic."

"Huh? Oh, right. Be careful. Those guys might still be hanging around."

"Yes. If it comes to that, I'll scream very loudly." Lebreau left the clinic lobby, disappearing down an inner corridor.

Who listened both to Isaac and the others talking and to Graham continuing to demolish the car outside.

Even though he couldn't have been more confused, he quietly shook his head before muttering to himself with a wry smile, trying to breathe out the nasty chill welling up inside him.

"What the heck is going on in this city…?"

⇔

Somewhere in New York   A room in a large hospital

At this hour, the sun wasn't quite up yet.

The single-occupant hospital room was exclusively for VIPs, but the man who lay on the bed was just a rank-and-file agent. The Bureau of Investigation had cut a deal with the hospital and had him placed in this room so they could talk about the top secret aspects of their inquiry in there.

"…I'm very sorry, Assistant Director Talbot."

The man in bed, Agent Edward Noah, had a bandaged face.

"Don't push yourself," Victor Talbot said, having just appeared in the doorway.

"No, I can talk without trouble. Breathing deeply or coughing makes my ribs ache, though."

"Then don't talk yourself hoarse, at least."

No doubt Edward was wrapped in bandages under the covers as well. He was black-and-blue all over, with multiple broken bones. Victor had heard it was going to take him at least six months to heal.

They said he hadn't even been conscious up until just twenty minutes ago.

Ordinarily, he wouldn't have been in any shape for visitors yet. However, Edward himself had requested this visit, and so Victor had come running over from the Bureau's New York investigation headquarters.

"Whaddaya think? Wishin' you'd drunk that elixir of immortality you seized from Szilard's boys?"

"Of course not." Edward had to be in terrible pain, but he smiled and answered easily. "If I were an immortal, I wouldn't be able to get time off this way. Aren't you the one who's jealous here, Assistant Director?"

"……Could be." Victor gazed out the window at the view.

Since Edward couldn't see his expression, he couldn't tell whether that had been a perfunctory response or whether he'd really meant it. After a short silence, he brought up the main topic. "Assistant Director... About the guys who jumped me..."

"Sorry. We've got an eyewitness report, but we haven't nabbed 'em yet," Victor said, lowering his gaze. Then he told Edward as much as he was able to: that a hat like Firo Prochainezo's had been found at the scene, as well as that it hadn't been evidence that Firo was the culprit but a warning aimed at him.

When he heard that, Edward smiled wryly. "Me? Of all people? He and I can't stand each other."

"Yeah, apparently the messenger was a complete dolt."

After that light exchange, Victor's tone went cold. "Rest easy. I'll make sure those screwballs swing for this."

"You aren't a judge. You don't have the authority for that, Assistant Director Talbot."

"Nobody was asking for sarcasm there."

His boss looked away, embarrassed, and this time Edward's face turned serious. He took a different angle. "...Have there been any developments with regard to the aircraft fire last night?"

"Nope. If I'd known this was gonna happen, I would have made you pull an all-nighter instead of telling you to get some rest."

As a matter of fact, most of Victor's men had worked all night, investigating that incident. However, he'd been planning to send Edward and a few others all around the port before this afternoon, so he'd ordered them to nap for a few hours. Since the investigation headquarters was cluttered and Edward lived nearby, he'd sent him back home. Now, that was a blunder he deeply regretted.

"You think Prochainezo's involved in that incident, too?"

"If it's okay to let my instincts do the talking, then yes, probably."

"Yeah, that's what I think, too. Actually, with immortals—well, with Huey being here in town, he may end up involved whether he wants to be or not. Not as many of us around these days, thanks to old Szilard."

Victor's remark sounded rather lonely.

"Assistant Director, every so often, it sounds as though you respect Szilard Quates."

"……"

"If it's hard to talk about, you don't have to."

"No… Frankly, back when Szilard started eating us on the boat, it was a shock, but…a part of me wasn't surprised at all. I didn't know anybody as greedy as that old guy. Knowledge, money, power—he took everything he could get."

Even Victor didn't seem to know how to arrange his face while he talked about this. He stared out the window, shifting through various expressions, smiling, then tensing. He probably thought he was hiding it, but the slightly grimy glass reflected him dimly, and Edward could see everything.

He didn't point this out, though. He just kept listening to what his boss said.

"The thing is, I appreciate that boundless greed of his. Respect it, too. I've got a habit of giving up on my own desires, see. Of course, I know the old guy wasn't right, not in the least. His greed was true to basic human instinct, and the only things that could stop it were products of human intelligence: the law and its organizations… Or that was what I figured anyway. Who'd have thought the old guy would get eaten by a young gangster punk…"

"It's the same thing. If Firo gets greedy, we'll deal with him. There's no difference."

"Dedicated, ain'cha." Victor smiled faintly, but his face was still turned toward the window, and he didn't let his subordinate see.

His boss's very human behavior almost elicited a sad smile from Edward, but he realized he hadn't finished stating his opinion, so he got back to being serious. "The guys who jumped me… Who do you think they were?"

"We're short on intel, but…probably Huey's henchmen from Larva or Time, or maybe Runorata flunkies; there are rumors he's teamed up with the syndicate. Or, as a dark horse, they could have been Senator Beriam's pet thugs."

Arbitrary assumptions weren't great, but Victor's men had thought these angles were likely, so they were investigating along those lines. However, since they couldn't think of a reason any of those factions would have a personal grudge against Firo, they hadn't made much headway.

"We checked into other people who might have a beef with the punk, but Szilard's former underlings must be pretty close to tapped out. I bet they think Maiza's the one who ate Szilard. I hear he also worked some of the local punks over real good. That Dallas kid was always saying he'd slaughter Firo one of these days."

"Dallas... Oh, he's just a thug; he's not worth bothering with. Although, I haven't seen him since I moved to my current post."

"So there's no way he would attack an agent like you, huh."

Nodding in agreement, Edward gave his own theory. "I only saw them in the moment after I fell, before I blacked out, but their shoes looked oddly expensive. It didn't seem as if they'd just hired local muscle."

"Yeah, these aren't your average goons. The guy who saw them run off said they were awfully well-dressed. That's where the theory about Beriam's pet thugs came from."

Edward paused to think. "This is just a hunch, but..."

"What?"

"The day before yesterday, we drew up a list of related organizations at that meeting, remember? I have a feeling the bunch who attacked me didn't belong to any of them."

"...Mind if I ask why?" Victor didn't tell him he was overthinking things. Instead, he prompted him to go on.

"It really is only a hunch, but... Their methods didn't seem to match the ones used by any of those groups. What would you call it...? Pointless provocation? Since we haven't met directly, I can't say for certain, but I didn't sense any of the aggressive weirdness Ladd Russo and the members of Lamia would have. The Nebula staff seems like the closest match, but something feels wrong about drawing that conclusion."

A dark shadow came into Edward's eyes. His tone was grave, filled with self-loathing over having abandoned the front line at a time like this.

"It's possible the roots of this incident go deeper than we're assuming."

Chapter 14   No One Knows the Future

There's something known as a lucid dream.

You're asleep and dreaming, but you're aware of these things.

In most cases, the moment you realize it's a dream, your blood pressure and level of awareness begin to change, and your body wakes up.

Whether it was because he'd just been slugged, or because he was very short on sleep, or due to some other factor, Nader Schasschule didn't know why he was in such a dream. The world would probably never know. In any case, he was sharply aware that none of this was real.

He could see an old, familiar set of swings.

Behind them, the cornfields of his hometown stretched as far as the eye could see.

Noticing that the roof of the barn that had burned down was still perfect and whole, Nader felt doubly sure this was a dream.

Creak...

     Creak...

       Creak...

Suddenly, he heard the sound of scraping iron behind him, but he wasn't particularly startled. He knew what it was from.

When he turned around, he saw a reversed version of the scene he'd just been looking at. In that mirror image, the swing was moving back and forth.

A girl was sitting on it.

"…Sonia, you…"

He muttered the name of his childhood friend, but the face of the girl on the swing was blurred.

He was afraid it might change into the Hilton-girl's face the way it had in his earlier dream, but Nader took a step closer to the swings.

"Nader, Nader. Listen. When are you going to become a hero for me?"

He was relieved this was a dream. If his actual friend had said this to him in real life, he knew it would have broken his heart.

"…Stop it," he said with a shake of his head, trying to reject her. Even though he knew he was dreaming, his heart was terribly weak, and he wasn't able to control how the dream went.

"Oh! Say, those people behind you are your friends, aren't they?! Nader, that's amazing! You really are a hero, huh!"

At the girl's words, Nader slowly turned around, but he vaguely knew what would be waiting for him.

Or maybe they appeared because he'd expected them to.

There were men in black suits, holding Thompsons.

The Lemures.

They'd been under Huey Laforet's command until Nader had gotten them to sell out their boss, then made them his own pawns.

Or that's how it should have gone.

The muzzles of countless guns turned his way, and his mind shut down.

Since he was dreaming, it hadn't technically "shut down." However— and there was no telling what part of his psychology was at work here—those guns weren't pointed at him. They were pointing at his childhood friend, the girl on the swing.

"Stop… Don't do it, fellas…"

"Stop what, Comrade Nader?"

"……!"

A voice echoed up from the ground at his feet, and in that instant, the color of the sky changed dramatically. So did the surrounding scenery.

The endless cornfields vanished, blotted out by a vast wasteland.

The swing and the girl were still there, though, standing alone on the railroad tracks that stretched away to the left and right, all the way to the horizon.

"This is what you wanted, isn't it?"

Against his will, his eyes were dragged down toward the voice at his feet.

A man in black was crawling there. His tongue lolled, nearly torn out of his mouth, and bright blood poured steadily from his lips, like a waterfall. It was Goose Perkins: the man who'd bitten through his own tongue and died, right in front of Nader, after the Flying Pussyfoot incident.

Not only had he lost his tongue, blood was gushing from his mouth, so there was no way he could really have talked. However, his voice reached Nader's ears clearly.

"That girl is in your way, isn't she?"

"No… It ain't like that…"

"What do you mean? If you can say 'it ain't like that' right away, Comrade Nader, it means you're already well aware of the reason she's in the way."

"Shut your mouth… You're dead. You know this is just a damn dream!"

He'd meant to shout, but the voice that made it out of his throat felt terribly thin.

"If she weren't here, no promises would bind you, and you could let go of your guilt." Goose's voice grew louder. Nader felt the swing start to shake and rattle.

A train was coming.

Maybe because it was a dream, he knew for sure what was going to happen next. They only took a moment to appear.

Enormous trains came barreling toward them from the left and right.

"If it weren't for her, no doubt you could just keep tricking and using people as you liked, and live a fairly good life."

"You're lying… I didn't… That's a lie…"

The trains were bearing down on them at an alarming speed, but if he ran to the girl on the swing now, he could save her. She seemed to be watching him and smiling, as if she hadn't even noticed the trains.

Even now, in the dream, Nader couldn't remember her face.

Despite that, he kicked Goose, who was crawling around by his feet, then broke into a run.

"It's no good. You won't make it in time. You only pretend you're giving your all," Goose said from where he lay sprawled on the dirt. Nader ignored him, and his feet pounded the ground. There was no sensation on the soles of his feet, only a vague sense of speed, of moving forward.

"Then you'll fool your swindling self, won't you, Comrade Nader? 'I did everything I could. I just couldn't beat fate.'"

"Shut up… Shut up!"

Blocking out Goose's voice, Nader stretched out his right hand.

Just one more step, and he'd reach the girl.

He could still make it.

If he caught her hand before she was crushed between the trains, if he pulled her to him, he was sure he'd remember her face.

A silver flash ran through his outstretched right hand.

"Oh…"

At that point, something came to mind—he didn't have a right hand that could reach for her.

Nader's hand fell off, and blood spurted from his wrist. Out of the corner of his eye, he saw a woman.

Unlike his childhood friend, this woman's face was very clear.

She was looking at him as if he were garbage. She shifted her grip on her enormous bloody knife—and with no hesitation, she slashed his throat.

Then the trains that were coming from either side crushed Nader's world.

$\Longleftrightarrow$

"Waaaaaaaaaaaaaaaaaugh!"

Screaming, he bolted up in bed.

Breathing roughly, Nader looked at his right wrist. The cheap-looking prosthetic hand was attached to it.

A dream.

Right, that was a dream…

He'd been aware of that all along, but the fact that it hadn't been real was still deeply reassuring.

Nader closed his eyes, trying to get his breathing under control. From a short distance away, a voice spoke to him.

"D-don't startle me like that… You okay?"

When he opened his blurry eyes a crack, he saw Roy.

Upham was standing behind him, watching Nader silently.

After waking from a dream like that one, though, he didn't have the energy to lunge at him the way he'd done earlier.

He seemed to be in his own room. How long had he been out? From the look of the light that filtered in through the window, it was probably a little past noon.

"Are you okay? For now, just calm down. All right?"

"…Yeah. I'm okay. I won't go ape on you again."

After Nader had spent a little while taking deep breaths, Roy spoke again. "While you were out cold… Uh, Upham told us about it. About that group you and he were in…the… What was it? The Lemures."

"…I see." Hiding the trembling that welled up from deep in his heart, Nader did his very best to sound tough. "So? Why aren't I dead? Is Huey gonna give you a reward if you bring me in alive?"

Upham sighed deeply, breaking his silence. "Look, I told you, it's not like that. We're in pretty similar positions, you and me."

"...Huh?"

"I left the Lemures, too. I deserted the other guys and booked it off that train. I hadn't heard any of the stuff you mentioned about Hilton, either. I've been lucky; nobody's found me yet."

"And I'm supposed to believe that?" Nader sounded skeptical.

Upham shrugged. "Since you're still alive, I'd say it's pretty credible."

"......"

Nader didn't completely buy it, but he remembered Upham had sounded worried about him earlier. After a short silence, he apologized. "Sorry about...all that earlier. You sold me out once, remember? We'll say this makes us even."

Nader was thinking of the group of black suits who had appeared in his dream.

He'd incited betrayal and had ended up being betrayed. He was remembering his few supporters being massacred.

The hostility was still there, but when Upham heard the word *even*, his expression softened a little, too. "Frankly, that's a big load off my mind. To tell you the truth, I figured you were still carrying a grudge against all of us in your coffin."

"...I already took that grudge out on Goose."

"? What do you mean?"

"I mean I don't have a beef with you people anymore. From what I hear, most of the Lemures got wiped out on that train. That bastard Goose was a pathetic cinder, lying on the tracks."

Nader was remembering the past as he spoke, but the creepy version of Goose from his nightmare flashed into his mind, and he went a little pale. After he'd taken a few more deep breaths, he turned to Roy. "Well, what are you going to do with me? Run me out of here?"

"I already told you, we've got plenty of fellas with stories they can't talk about here. If you still think we might sell you out, go buy yourself a better lock for your door," Roy said. There was a little irony in his voice.

Nader sounded suspicious. "You know about me now. Why harbor a failed terrorist? What's in it for you?"

"If you're paying rent, well, we get that out of it." Roy gave a self-mocking smile, then spoke to both Nader and Upham. "Anything's fine. I'm not the cops, and with my past, I'd rather they didn't look at me too closely, either."

Yeah, I bet that past involves dope. Nader already knew that, but he didn't press Roy for details. The guy might not look exactly healthy, but from the way he talked, his days as a junkie seemed to be behind him.

Having made that call, Nader started thinking about what came next.

What do I do now? Should I lie low here until the Hilton bitches give up? ...Until when? How long should I hide?

She's everywhere. I hid in the pen for three years, and even then, she— Actually, what is that Hilton group anyway? How did she know my face? Is there a photo making the rounds?

It had taken some time, but now that he'd calmed down, various questions started to rear their heads.

If that waitress had run into him completely by accident, why had Hilton been dressed like that? Was she spying while working as a waitress? On that thought, Nader decided to give Roy and Upham a description of her and ask where she might be waiting tables.

Even though he hadn't expected much, Roy gave him the answer easily. "Oh, if the uniform was that color, she's probably at Alveare."

"...Alveare?"

Upham picked up where Roy had left off. "It's the biggest restaurant in Little Italy. I'm pretty sure it's run by this small outfit called the Martillo Family."

"The Martillos?"

You mean the ones from that casino yesterday...?

......

...What is this? What's going on?

Generally speaking, Nader wasn't particularly skilled.

However, in just a few years, he'd worked his way up as a con man, then fallen all the way to the abyss of death, and that experience stirred up a strange, unpleasant feeling inside him. He sensed a weird "connection" between these events, and cold sweat broke out on his back.

He also knew he wasn't at the center of the connections.

He felt as if he'd just happened to pass by some sort of chain of incidents.

Was he standing next to an enormous current that swallowed his own attempts to flee? He wanted to think it was an illusion, but he couldn't get that cold sense of foreboding out of his head.

In purely personal terms, as a swindler who'd spent long years in underworld society, Nader sensed the definite presence of "currents" that logic couldn't explain. Not minor currents, like a winning streak or a run of bad luck. Large currents, like destiny… Long story short, he was confident in his ability to sense whether the organization he belonged to was on its way up or heading downhill.

The one time he'd ignored that current, he'd lost his right hand and been forced to live the wretched life of a man on the run.

He had the overwhelming feeling he was in the midst of that sort of current again. He sensed the presence of it beside him. While it probably wouldn't rouse the nation to action, it was more than big enough to crush a single organization. It was a torrent like none he'd ever felt before, and it sent a shudder through him; he didn't know whether it would spell good luck or bad for him.

It was so vast that he couldn't even tell which direction destiny was flowing.

Say my hunch is right on the money.

What should I do? Should I make a break for it so I don't get pulled into that current? Or should I ride that current to make my getaway?

The question was, what sort of situation was it for Hilton and the rest of Huey's people? That was important, but simply trying to suss it out could get him killed.

If the Martillo Family and Huey's faction were tangling with each other somehow, he should probably hope Huey's organization would be crushed. However, he couldn't see one of New York's smallest gangs managing to pull that off.

Argh, dammit.

What am I supposed to do?

After he'd been silent for a bit, Roy spoke to him with a little smile. "I dunno what you're worrying about, but… Do you have family?"

"…No."

"What about a girl or an old pal?"

"…Yeah…well…"

Nader was thinking of his childhood friend, the girl who'd turned up in his dream.

"Don't neglect your ties to other people. If you accidentally step off the path and end up in deep trouble, sometimes they'll pull you back out. That's how I kicked the dope habit."

"…Sometimes those ties can bind you so tight you can't move, too. There's nothing wrong with being a lone wolf."

"Mm, true. I just figured if you needed to talk this over with someone else, somebody you were close to might be better than Upham and me."

"Oh… I see, yeah. Sorry."

That should have been the end of the conversation, but Nader was wondering what his friend was doing now. When he'd returned to his hometown, she'd already been gone. The Hiltons couldn't have done something to her, could they?

I know. I'll look for her.

If I see Sonia…something might change.

However, if he met her now, wouldn't he end up pulling her into his life on the run?

Right, so I don't need to see her.

No, that's just an excuse.

Two opposing thoughts popped into his head. However, Nader knew they were nothing as noble as an angel and devil. It was just his sorry selves, which couldn't become either fully good or fully evil, yelling at each other.

He found himself staring at his prosthetic right hand.

He wanted the courage to reach out for something.

A hand that could pull her close would be fine.

One that would push her away from him would be fine, too.

Whether he chose to ride the vast current that swirled around him or run from it, nothing would happen at all if he didn't get moving.

He only wanted a small sign.

It could be a current as tiny as the ripples created by a frog jumping into a pond; he didn't care. If he had a current to push him forward...

No... That's not it.

Really, I'm just looking for an excuse not to move.

Nader didn't have the energy to start a wave of his own anymore. He vaguely suspected he might just stagnate here forever, rotting away while he was still alive.

That prediction was on the verge of coming at least half true.

Nader was forgetting something, though.

He'd already been pulled into the current of the crazy ruckus four years back.

The conversation with Roy and Upham had trailed off, leaving Nader feeling awkward. He smacked his cheeks, trying to wake himself up—and then he felt something strange.

Huh? What's...? Bandages?

His head and face had been properly treated and wrapped in bandages. A few places hurt when he touched them. Maybe he'd cut himself when he'd passed out.

"Did you fellas patch me up?"

"Huh? Oh, no, no way! We just put pressure on your wounds. The doc's the one who checked you over and bandaged you! He came by around noon to introduce some new cargo movers. It seemed like perfect timing, so we asked him to help with you."

"Oh... Guess I'll have to pay him."

"Nah, don't worry about it."

"You know I can't just mooch like that."

Nader didn't want to put himself in someone else's debt. He figured he'd take a few bills out of his pillow once the other two had left the room.

However, Roy kept shaking his head. "Really, he doesn't need it. He said it was like a follow-up."

"?"

"Sheesh, c'mon. If you already knew the doc, you shoulda said something."

"Huh?" Nader didn't get it, and his eyes went round.

What are they talking about?

I don't know any doctors...

But before he finished that thought, he realized something.

Wait. I do know one.

But, no... It can't be, right?

Through his confusion, Nader heard the door beside him open.

"Hey, doc! Nader's awake!" Roy spoke up cheerfully. Nader automatically glanced in that direction.

A man who seemed far too faded for the occasion of a "miraculous reunion" was standing there.

"Hello. How are you feeling, Nader?"

"————!" Speechless, Nader stared at the other man.

He wore gray fabric from head to toe. Even his face was covered with a gray turban and muffler.

A gray magician.

That was the impression most people got when they saw him for the first time. Nader had been no exception.

That said, the *first* time he'd met him, because of the circumstances, he'd thought of something else.

On that day, the burns from the explosion and all the blood he'd lost had left him at death's door.

As he crawled across the parched earth, when he encountered the man in gray, he genuinely thought the grim reaper had come for him.

And perhaps in a way, the man was some incarnation of death.

But he wasn't there to take his life. He'd come to tell him, "Your time hasn't come yet."

Then he remembered.

He hadn't exactly forgotten this particular fact, but it had been submerged at the bottom of his heart all this time.

He'd already died once.

After nearly throwing away his life through a series of stupid mistakes, he'd been saved only thanks to this passerby.

"Well, well. Destiny really does exist, I see," the gray magician muttered.

Before Nader knew it, tears were welling in his eyes. "You… Why're you here?"

He didn't know why the mere coincidence of their reunion was making him cry. The one thing he did know was that, just now, he'd been given a very definite push *forward*.

Will this…work? he thought. *You mean I'm not actually all washed up yet?*

Fortune was finally going his way.

His pretentiousness as a small-timer had once backed him into a fatal corner, but now it was working in an extremely positive way, as the driving force that would propel him back up from the depths he'd sunk into.

No, believe in it. What's the point of not believing in this?

Yeah, I'm sure this great "current" is going to end up working in my favor.

At this point, he had the feeling that whatever he did would go well. *I bet the era's mine, ain't it?*

Nader was on the verge of believing this, but in only a few seconds, the universe put a damper on that.

From behind the gray magician, a familiar face spoke with a voice he knew. "Hey, Nader! Haven't seen you for half a day, pal."

Ladd Russo, who was standing behind Fred, wore a fiendish smile. When Nader saw him, he thought he must still be dreaming.

Unfortunately, no matter how long he waited, he didn't wake up.

$\Longleftrightarrow$

Thirty minutes later   The dining hall

Nader's mood had crashed again. He'd ended up listening to Ladd in the room for a long, long time after Roy and the rest had stepped out.

According to Ladd, the clinic where his so-called old friend worked was owned by Fred, the gray magician.

"That was a shock. Who'd have figured ol' Who had gotten off the train with that magician fella in one piece...

"Not only that, but I met up with a guy I knew in stir there. Small world, ain't it?!

"And then you and I met up again, too."

That was what he'd learned from Ladd's careless explanation. However, what concerned Nader was the money he'd been given to use at the casino.

As it turned out, though, there was nothing to worry about.

"Huh? Oh, that. That's fine. The mazuma's yours, eh?"

It had been quite a sum, but Ladd talked about it like it was nothing. That made Nader's knees go weak.

For a little while after that, he told Ladd what he'd wanted to know about his connection to the Flying Pussyfoot incident.

In other words, Nader told him what Upham had told Roy earlier. It would have been easier to talk about with Upham present, but apparently the guy was also a technical worker, and he'd gone to work on some interior finishing construction elsewhere in the building.

Now he'd finished his story, and Ladd was grinning at him. "Huey, huh? Nice, nice. I didn't expect to find another connection to that guy here... Still, there's no way a flunky like you would know where his hideout is, huh."

Ladd sounded half delighted and half disappointed, and Nader was quietly relieved.

I thought he might beat me to death if we met again... Who'd have thought he knew that doctor? He may be a better guy than I figured.

The people with him, too... That fella in the coveralls is one thing, but the two who came with him today seem pretty laid-back.

Forming a drastic misconception about Ladd, Nader glanced at the corridor. The door to his room was standing open, and he could hear people talking out in the hall.

"Let me tell you a sad, sad story."

As Graham delivered the usual line, the man and woman who were with him protested.

"Huh?! No, don't! No sad stories!"

"If you tell sad stories, your happiness runs away!"

"Make it a fun story!"

"Yes, or a funny story!"

Graham had never gotten that particular response before, and he fell to thinking. "Tell a fun story, when I'm feeling this sad? God's given me another tall order. Wait... You're the ones who gave me that tall order, so... You're God?!"

At this insane switchback from Graham, the man and woman—Isaac and Miria—cried out in astonishment.

"What?! Is that true, Miria?! Are we gods?!"

"Oh my God!"

"I see... I hadn't picked up on that. But where are we the gods of?"

"Maybe Japan. Mr. Yaguruma said they have eight million of them there."

What the heck is with these guys? Shaft thought as he watched the pair have a serious discussion about a nonsense topic. However, the talk promptly turned his way.

"A fun story... A story fun enough to offer to the gods... What to do...? They say a certain religion in some country offered sacrifices to their gods to put 'em in a good mood, but all I've got to offer is Shaft... So I guess Shaft over there is gonna tell you a funny story that's guaranteed to have you holding your stomachs and rolling in the aisles."

"You've gotta be kidding me!" Shaft yelled.

"If it isn't funny, I'll bend all your joints in fun directions. How about that?!"

"How about *no*! Why do I have to be a sacrifice?!"

Isaac flashed him a thumbs-up. "No worries. Think positive! If he's offering you as a sacrifice to the gods, it means you're important to him! Like his son or a goat!"

"Yes, seven kids for Abraham!"

"Sons and goats are pretty different!"

"Relax, Shaft. Man or goat, I'll always keep you at my beck and call!"

Hearing bits of the conversation in the corridor, Nader felt a sincere envy for the group.

Wow... They just seem so...dumb and carefree. Lucky...

Nader's thoughts waxed uncharacteristically sentimental. He wondered if they'd keep going through life their own way, without even noticing the nationwide suffering the Depression was causing.

He might have felt this way because their easygoing manner reminded him vaguely of his childhood friend.

Listening to them, he might even be able to remember her face clearly.

Ladd muttered, "Okay, so what's our next move?" and fell to thinking. Nader took that as an opportunity and tried to fill his mind with memories of his hometown.

His efforts were shut down by a racket that echoed up from the first floor.

⟺

The lodging house   First floor

The angry shouts, laughter, and metallic clangs they'd started to hear on the lower floor got everyone's attention, and the people who'd been near Nader's room all went downstairs.

Nader was the first to peek into the dining hall. When he saw the face that was in there, though, he hastily ducked back into the shadows of the corridor.

I'm pretty sure he was...

They hadn't talked, but he recognized those eyes, as sharp as knives.

He was at the casino with the manager—that Firo kid!

"Calm down, please, Mr. Smith."

Smith responded to Luck Gandor without looking at him. "Tell that to this little girl."

The "little girl" was a woman who was staring him down from just ten centimeters away and dressed like she'd just stepped out of a saloon. At the moment, she was trying to slash Smith in two, right down the middle, with a pair of Japanese katanas. Smith had blocked them with the pistols he held in both hands. Neither could afford to back down.

Impassively, Luck said, "You drew first, Mr. Smith."

"Well, sure I did. If you're here at all, you're obviously after my head," Smith grunted.

Maria, the woman with the katanas, laughed at him. "Ah-ha-ha-ha-ha! You're a total genius as always, amigo! What would Luck want with the head of a sissy like you?!"

"Why you little—!"

"What do we have here? It looks like a whole lotta fun... Wait, is that that idiot Smith?"

"Let me tell you a fun story... That is most definitely Mr. Smith. I see... They say Japanese katanas were forged as offerings to the gods sometimes. In other words, Smith is trying to get katanas to use as offerings for Shaft and me?! Could there be a happier story?!"

"Actually, that guy over there was at Firo's casino yesterday."

Ladd and Graham had taken a look into the dining hall and were discussing what they'd seen. However, Nader was hiding in the shadows of the corridor, and he couldn't check on what was happening inside.

Roy, who'd also glanced into the dining hall, came over to Nader and whispered, "That's Mr. Luck. Luck Gandor."

"...Who's he?"

"One of the fellas who supports this place. Publicly, he passes himself off as the manager of a jazz hall, but he's the boss of a little outfit called the Gandor Family. See, my girl works at that jazz hall. He's

helped me out a few times. He's not an out-and-out villain…or that's what I'd like to tell you, but the mafia's the mafia, y'know."

"Yet another syndicate, huh?"

What the hell is this?! One after another…! Internally, Nader was screaming.

In the dining hall, Luck calmly continued talking.

"Maria."

The girl with the katanas answered Luck without turning around. "What is it, amigo? Where do you want me to slash this guy?"

"Take back the fact that you called him a sissy and apologize, please."

"Huh? But…"

"No buts." He spoke as if he was scolding a child, but his words held a sharp-edged pressure.

Maria sulked, puffing out her cheeks. Then she lowered her katanas and bowed her head. "Argh… Sorry, amigo. Didn't mean it. You're not a sissy."

"Why you… Do you actually think a careless apology like that will quell my insanity?" Smith complained.

His young apprentice cut in from beside him. "I think you should prove you're the bigger man and back down, Master," he whispered, and Smith grudgingly lowered his guns.

Beside them, an old man was taking gulps from a bottle of liquor. He was spreading a boozy stink around, and the ruckus didn't seem to have fazed him.

In the midst of that chaos, Luck spoke with calm self-possession. He was talking not just to Smith but to the liquored-up old guy as well. "Mr. Smith, Mr. Alkins. There is a job I would like your help with."

In response to Luck's businesslike proposal, Smith's eyebrows came together, while Alkins's eyes widened slightly, although he kept his lips on the liquor bottle.

Then Luck began to explain briefly.

He told them about the casino opening that would be held at Ra's Lance in the middle of February and that the Runorata Family was acting behind the scenes. He also mentioned that there was a possibility things would get rough there, although he didn't go into detail, and that he wanted to hire a few free agents who could move more easily than his syndicate.

Once he finished, the reaction was dubious. "...I don't buy this. You could just hire some random local punks to fill out your ranks." Alkins delivered a sound argument with boozy breath, but Luck quietly shook his head.

"In an ordinary conflict between mafia syndicates, that would be possible. No... In that case, our family would be enough on its own."

"Hoh! Get a load of you."

"However, these circumstances are rather extraordinary. That is why I came to you two..." At that point, Luck broke off for a moment, glancing at the boy who stood beside Smith.

Seeming to realize what that look meant, Smith explained, "This is my first apprentice. Someday, he'll inherit all my insanity. You can say anything in front of him. If you don't trust him, you don't trust me."

"...Very well. It's not the sort of story ordinary people would believe anyway." Making his decision based on the look in the boy's eyes, rather than what Smith had said, Luck went on. "There's a possibility this incident involves the immortals."

At those words, the boy flinched.

Luck found his reaction a little unexpected.

He didn't know that the kid had once marched into the Gandor Family office and smashed a bottle of the "failed" elixir that Szilard had left behind. He'd been given a report on the incident itself, of course, but since he hadn't met the boy in person, he hadn't connected him with the one who was in front of him now.

Although that reaction tugged at him, Luck kept his poker face firmly in place. "This is only a possibility, but... The terrorist Huey Laforet may be involved as well."

He'd based that particular remark on information Firo had given him. This time, it was the rubberneckers who were peeking into the dining hall who reacted.

"...Huey Laforet?" Nader's spine creaked.

Is he saying Huey's outfit is going to be in on that casino party or whatever it is?

Is that it...?

Is that what's been giving me this weird, uneasy feeling?

"...Huey Laforet?" Ladd ground his molars.

I never figured I'd hear that name in a place like this.

A casino, huh...? That ginger bastard and the Melvi gink are gonna turn up there, too, aren't they?

So if I play my cards right, I'll be able to butcher all three of 'em at once!

"Wait. Before any of that, do you actually think we'd take a job from the Gandors?"

"'Slong as I can pick up likker money, I'll take it. I'll pass up the chance to go a coupla rounds with Vino fer now," Alkins slurred.

"Gah... Play along a little, would you, Gramps?" Smith said.

Overhearing their conversation, Luck decided to keep the fact that Vino had gone over to the enemy under wraps for a while longer. Sighing, he went on. "Quite true. Taking a job from an organization that was once your enemy isn't something sane people do. No hitman who wanted to live a steady, peaceful life would accept an offer like this one."

"......" Smith's nose twitched.

Seeing that, his apprentice thought, *Oh, he's going to take this job.* He was certain how this would end now, but he didn't dare say a word.

"That is exactly why I came to you, Mr. Smith. I've heard you are in possession of a sense of aesthetics regarding your profession that transcends common sense. View my offer from this perspective, if you would: I've come to you not as an individual but to pay my respects to your...well, insane conviction toward your work."

"Oh-ho-ho..." Smith had tried for a brusque response, but his lips began to curve in a happy smirk. Still holding his guns, he tried to push his mouth back into a stoic expression as he responded. "I see. You've got promise. That said, it's not enough to hear rumors and imagine. Once you've seen me at work, you yourself will be taken in by true insani— Gwuff?!"

In the middle of his sentence, Smith took a kick to the back and pitched forward.

"Aaaargh… Dammit, who was that?!" Clearly furious, he turned around—and there was Ladd, wearing a vicious smile. "Wha…? Ladd?! Why are you here?!"

"Damn, fella, you always phrase things in the worst way. I bet you're thinking you're all special and you're gonna live forever." Ladd jerked a thumb at Graham, who stood behind him, while turning toward Smith with deadly intent. "I only spared your life on account of Kid Graham looking up to you, remember?"

"Intriguing… Do you wish to be the clown who gets killed by the life he spared?" Slowly, Smith raised his gun.

However, Ladd ignored him and turned to Luck. "I overheard all that. You say you're looking for guys with skills?"

"You're…" Naturally, Luck knew about Ladd. Even leaving out the fact that he was Firo's acquaintance, there was no way he could have forgotten him after seeing him raise hell at the casino the night before.

"See, I'm looking for work myself. I think I could be pretty useful. You're a pal of Firo's, right? I'll give you a friends-and-family discount. You can pay me half of whatever you pay that fool Smith."

"……"

For a little while, Luck was silent.

In for a penny, in for a pound, he'd thought. That was why he'd come to scout his former enemies, but he had never imagined this man would be here.

Even if that commotion the previous day had been all he'd seen, he would have been able to tell—the guy was strong, but he was also dangerous.

Forget a pound; it would be like betting the entire bank.

However, after giving it another several seconds of careful consideration, Luck steeled himself. "If we determine you're a maverick, remember we'll dispose of you, even if it means you kill us in the struggle."

"…Ha! I like it! You're ready to face death; I can see it in your eyes. I love that," Ladd said.

Luck made sure not to let his feelings show, but he found the comment plenty amusing. *Prepared to die? Now that I'm immortal? I thought I'd lost that… But I can't imagine this man has misread me.*

Just a few hours ago, I was almost killed by another right hand. Perhaps my old senses have begun to return.

Even as these thoughts ran through his mind, Luck drew a deep breath, then spoke to the hitmen, Ladd included. "For now, I would like all of you to stop by the Gandors' office.

"Understand that the moment you step inside, it will be *too late* to turn back."

⇔

Evening   Millionaire's Row, the Genoard family's second residence

"Still… Even if the protection money for the Martillo Family is all taken care of, what are we going to do about living expenses in the meantime?"

Jacuzzi gave Nice a self-deprecating smile. "We don't have much choice. I hate to do it, but let's look for a buyer for this wine."

Jacuzzi was holding the top-drawer wine that Eve Genoard had given them the other day. He didn't feel great about selling a gift, but necessity knew no law.

He took a bottle of wine out of the box and started for the entryway, cradling it in his arms. "Since we've been introduced and all, I'll ask if the restaurant that Mr. Martillo runs will buy it."

"I'll go with you this time. I'd like to see what sort of place it is."

As they were talking, the pair had descended to the front entrance, but then the doorbell rang, and they heard a familiar voice from outside.

"Excuse me. Is anyone there?"

At the sound of the voice, the two of them exchanged a glance. Jacuzzi hastily hid the wine behind a vase. Without meaning to, he'd started acting suspicious. Meanwhile, Nice remained perfectly calm and opened the front door wide.

The girl who stood there was as lovely as her sweet voice had suggested. A car was stopped in front of the gate, and an elderly man in a butler's uniform and the plump Black woman who worked as the housekeeper stood beside it.

"Oh! Jacuzzi and Nice. We haven't seen each other in quite some time, have we? Um, the wine I sent you the other day didn't cause you any trouble, did it?"

"N-no! Absolutely not the tiniest little bit of it at all ever! Uh-uh!" Jacuzzi's voice trembled as his anxiety mingled with guilt. He didn't seem to know where to look.

Meanwhile, Nice greeted the girl respectfully. "Yes, it's been a very long time, Miss Eve. We're very grateful for all you do for us."

"Ah-ha-ha. Please, Nice, don't be so formal." The girl smiled. Unlike Jacuzzi and the others, she carried herself in a way that suited the luxury residential neighborhood of Millionaire's Row very well.

This was Eve Genoard.

She was the mansion's rightful owner and the "employer" who was letting Jacuzzi's group stay here in exchange for maintaining it. Technically, this was her second residence, but her sudden visit flustered Jacuzzi.

Noticing that the girl's smile had clouded over slightly, he asked her a timid question. "U-um… Is something the matter?"

Eve responded with a question of her own, seeming just a little more concerned than usual about the people around them. "Well… Excuse my abruptness, but my brother Dallas hasn't been here, has he?"

Jacuzzi and Nice exchanged looks again.

As Eve had guessed—

—Dallas had been in this mansion just a few hours earlier.

"You fellas be my backers. If I win at the casino, I'll pay you back the principal, plus ten percent."

The owner of the mansion had appeared out of nowhere and made high-handed demands.

Of course, as far as Jacuzzi's group was concerned, Eve was the mansion's owner, so they treated Dallas as a nuisance. When the delinquents told him they were all flat broke, his mood had soured instantly.

"The hell?! Not one red cent? Tch! Useless! Dammit, looking at your bankrupt faces is gonna take my luck down a few pegs, too. Later, suckers!"

With that rude rejoinder, he'd snatched up a few clocks, dishes, and other items that seemed likely to sell for a good price, then left.

When they told Eve what had happened, she heaved a sigh. "Um… I'm terribly sorry my brother made trouble for you."

"Oh, no, no! It's fine—we're used to it!" Jacuzzi said.

"Jacuzzi!" Nice scolded him in a whisper.

With a gasp, Jacuzzi caught himself. "Oh! No, uh, th-th-th-that's not what I meant! It's not like he's causing trouble for us constantly or anything like that; it's just…"

"It's all right. I know my brother does make a nuisance of himself to all sorts of people. I've asked him to stop again and again, but…"

Dallas was a skunk, but he loved his little sister. He was probably pulling the wool over her eyes by acting as if he'd reformed when he was around her.

That was what Jacuzzi thought anyway, but he didn't say so. Instead, he asked a simple question. "But why would Mr. Dallas *also* be going to the casino event?"

"Also?"

"Oh, uh, just a figure of speech. Please don't worry about it."

It was probably better not to mention that they'd be going to the casino opening as well. Eve worried a lot to begin with, and they might end up dragging her into trouble she didn't need. Putting her off in an absent way, Jacuzzi prompted her to go on.

According to Eve, other wealthy citizens—particularly those with connections to the Runorata Family—had received invitations, which had been distributed extravagantly, one for each individual rather than one per family.

"The Runorata Family killed my father and oldest brother, and yet they sent us invitations… I have to admit I was angry. Only two invitations were sent to our house: one for myself and one for Dallas. They knew we were the only two remaining members of our family, and they invited us anyway."

"That's…really awful."

"I was furious, but for some reason, my brother was very keen on it. He said, 'When casinos open, they want to rope in regular customers, so they make the jackpots easier to hit.' He took most of the cash we had on hand and left the house…"

"Yikes…"

When they heard this, both Jacuzzi and Nice thought, *Same as ever; that guy couldn't be any scummier,* but of course they didn't say it aloud.

After that, Jacuzzi and the others promised to contact Eve if they saw Dallas, then waved as she left.

They exchanged looks, but for a little while, none of them said a word.

Then, unable to take the silence any longer, Nick spoke up timidly. "So, uh… That means Dallas is gonna be there on the day, too, right?"

At that, the delinquents started whispering among themselves.

("…What'll we do if we run into him? He'll rip us a new one for playing when we didn't give him any dough.")

("We can just tell 'em we borrowed ours from the Martillos.")

("Aah, Dallas hate Firo from Martillos. He said someday he kill.")

("Hey, whoa, what happens to us if he finds out we're helping Firo?")

("He might shank us.")

("If he does, we'll settle his hash instead.")

("But that guy can't die, can he?")

("That's okaaay. We can just bury him alive somewheeere.")

("Sometimes you say some real scary stuff, Melody.")

("If we buried him, Eve would cry.")

("I'll be Eve's big brother instead, so that part's fine.")

("Shut yer yap." "Die." "Fade." "Take a bunk.")

("Hya-haah?" "Hya-haw!")

His friends were the same as always, but Jacuzzi looked even wearier than usual. Turning to Nice, he spoke very quietly so that only she would hear. "...Sorry, Nice. It looks like we've got more trouble."

"Don't worry, Jacuzzi. If it comes down to it, I'll blow all our troubles away." Nice winked, but since she was wearing an eye patch, it just looked like she was smiling with her eyes shut.

"That actually makes me feel worse...but thanks anyway, Nice."

They'd had many similar exchanges, but for that very reason, the familiarity made Jacuzzi happy.

He wanted things to be peaceful at night, at least, while he was with his friends.

This modest wish of Jacuzzi's was shattered just a few minutes later by the strident sound of the doorbell.

"I'm home."

When they opened the front door, Rail was standing there.

That in itself wasn't a problem at all, but the man standing nearby certainly was.

"Hi there! Haven't seen you since yesterday! How've you been, Ink?! I like that tattoo of yours. It's as if you're rebelling against the body your parents gave you! Open hostility toward Nature! How fun!"

Jacuzzi couldn't keep up with Christopher's energy. Moving stiffly, he turned to look at Rail.

"Oh, he said he didn't have anywhere to go. Put him up for the night, all right? We're all going to be doing the same job, and this way it'll be easier to talk things over before we get started. That's good, isn't it?" Rail said, casually taking charge.

Jacuzzi wished something would blow him to kingdom come.

But the situation wasn't entirely hopeless.

"I'm sorry to barge in on you like this."

Ricardo appeared from behind Christopher and offered him one saving grace:

"As our rent, please let us cover the food expenses of everyone who lives here."

⇔

Night   In front of the Runorata villa

"Well, that's another day's work done."

After escorting Melvi back to the villa, Claire had gone to see Huey, who was on the same property. He'd talked with him about Chané until nightfall and had then walked out through the gate.

Apparently, Huey was here to meet with the Runoratas.

My father-in-law, Huey the terrorist, and the Runorata Family, huh?

I'm curious about that combination, but whatever. I'll ask Chané about it later when we've got the time.

Chané was off doing some sort of job on her own, and he hadn't seen her since meeting Huey. According to what Huey had just told him, every time he'd brought up the subject of Claire, Chané's expression had cycled through a fascinating kaleidoscope of emotion.

Yeah, I want to go see her right now. I have to let her know I told her dad I intend to marry her.

Well, to make that happen, I'll have to guard that crumb until this job's over.

On that thought, he decided to patrol the wall's outer perimeter before going home. He was off the clock, but he figured he'd give them a little bonus and make sure nobody suspicious was hanging around.

Of course, he thought there probably weren't many people who knew this was the Runorata Family villa and were still reckless enough to get near the place.

As it turned out, though, that assumption was proven false right off the bat.

When he reached the narrow alley around back, he spotted a woman. She'd piled up nearby trash cans and rocks, and she was struggling to get over the wall.

"Whoa…," he muttered. *Who'd have thought anybody would be*

trying something this blatantly suspicious? A little appalled, he went over to the woman.

She had a terrific figure and was dressed very well, but he really couldn't believe she had any legitimate connection to the villa. She also didn't look young enough to be the Runorata's daughter, breaking curfew.

"Uh, hey, miss?" He really doubted she was here to bump off Melvi, but she was definitely suspicious. "A scary mafia guy owns this villa. If you're planning to steal something, I'd hit up an undiscovered ancient ruin or sunken ship instead. Nobody's gonna call the cops on you there."

His advice for the trespasser wasn't quite on target, though.

"What? You don't say! Oh, but I'm not planning to rob them. It just sounds as though the person I'm looking for is in here..."

The woman turned around. She didn't seem particularly flustered, but when he saw her face, he froze.

"Hmm?"

"Yes?" She looked puzzled.

He observed the woman's face by the light of the moon and the distant streetlights. "The shape of your ears and the line of your nose..."

"Pardon?"

"You wouldn't happen to be...Chané's big sister?!"

The remark was so ridiculous that anyone who knew even a little about the situation would have doubted their ears.

"What?! By 'Chané,' do you mean Miss Chané Laforet?"

"Yes."

The woman gave him an easygoing answer:

"Um, if you're asking how we're related, I'm not her sister. *I'm her mother...*"

"Her mother! Wow, you're really young!" Claire handled this extremely abrupt encounter in the exact same way he'd dealt with Huey. "I'm Felix Walken. It's an honor to meet you."

"I see... I'm Renee."

The woman looked perplexed; she seemed to be wondering why he'd suddenly introduced himself. Claire took her hand. "Really, thank you, ma'am. Thank you so much for bringing Chané into my world!"

"Huh?!"

"Your daughter is graciously allowing me to court her. Frankly, I don't think marriage is too far off."

Chané and Huey resembled each other, but this woman didn't look much like her daughter. Even so, although it wasn't clear whether it had been due to his remarkable observational skills or his love for Chané, he'd managed to spot even that slight genetic similarity.

The one sure thing was that Claire was very, very different.

However, even in the presence of that "abnormal human specimen," Renee didn't look the slightest bit surprised. She only observed him as if she were examining a rare mushroom. He was utterly intriguing to her. Abruptly, she realized something. "Hmm? Um, listen… If you're going to marry Chané, does that mean you'll live together?"

"Of course. I'm thinking of building us a house with an ocean view."

"Then you'll be together all the time, you mean."

"Until death do us part… Actually, I'm planning to stay together even after that."

Claire wasn't joking or anything. He was serious.

Troubled, Renee said, "Hmm. That's very odd. Huey said he'd give one of them to me. I wonder if he meant the other one we made, then."

"?"

"One of my reasons for coming here was to claim Chané, but… Um, Felix, was it? Does Huey Laforet know you're going to marry her?"

"Yes." Claire nodded firmly, filling her in on their "contract." "Father—I mean, Huey said if I helped him out with a job, he'd gladly accept my marriage to Chané."

"Oh dear, did he really…? Hmm. That's a problem. How inconsiderate of him. Then I suppose he really did mean the other one…"

As he watched the woman mutter to herself, Claire thought, *I see. They must be arguing over who gets custody of their daughter.*

I wonder if they divorced. And here Chané's grown and out on her own already.

These were common-sense guesses, but they were extremely off base.

Come to think of it, Chané talks about her old man a lot, but I've never heard her talk about her old lady.

He thought they must have some pretty complicated family circumstances, but naturally, that didn't change his feelings for his beloved.

After worrying and looking troubled for a while, the woman turned to Claire. "Let's do this, then. It's all right if it's only while you're working for Huey. Would you help me out with *my* job as well? If you will, while I do feel it's a shame, I'll let you have Chané."

She was clearly treating her daughter like an object, and that was concerning. Maybe when you'd had a kid, they seemed like a part of you, since you'd gone through labor for them.

It did tug at him a bit, but when it came to the human heart, Claire had no common sense. His guess was enough to satisfy him, so he spoke confidently to the mother of the woman he loved.

"Just you leave it to me. After all, for me, nothing's impossible."

⇔

Night   The Genoard residence, somewhere in New Jersey

"Dallas..."

Back home, Eve was still worried about her only brother.

He was practically never home anyway, but the Runorata Family was involved this time, and they'd killed their family. Even if Dallas couldn't actually die, if they stuffed him in an oil drum again and put him at the bottom of a river somewhere, she might never find him.

The surest bet would be to take her own invitation and go directly to the casino to look for him. However, since her brother had taken almost all the cash in the house, she might not be able to pay the entrance fee. Even if she had an invitation, if she couldn't buy the minimum number of chips, they might run her out.

More importantly, would she be able to search for him properly if she didn't know the first thing about casinos? Her invitation said she could bring a companion, but Eve couldn't think of anyone who'd really know their way around a casino.

Or rather, she did know someone, but she certainly couldn't invite him—Luck Gandor.

He'd know about casinos, and it would probably be easy for him to look for her brother. However, Dallas had done something unforgivable to him.

Eve's reluctance was partly because she really couldn't see him cooperating with her, but she also wasn't shameless or cruel enough to ask him for help with this. She'd considered asking for advice, at least, but even that would be brazen. She couldn't do it.

And what is Dallas planning to do if he runs into any of the Gandor men? This is a mafia get-together, so they certainly might be there...

Eve had direct personal knowledge of the fact that the Runoratas and the Gandors had been at war at one point, and so she really didn't expect the Gandors to be present. However, she also knew that, in this world, there was no such thing as "never." After all, a few years ago, even her common-sense assumption that "people inevitably die" had been turned on its ear.

That said, Eve was *neither strong nor weak enough* to write off her brother completely and say that he'd been asking for whatever trouble happened to break out around him.

What could she do?

She would have grasped at any straw that presented itself.

Just as she was thinking this, her butler, Benjamin, knocked on the door of her room. "Miss, a strange fellow says he needs to speak with you."

"With me?"

"He says it's about the Runorata casino... Shall I ask him to leave?"

"! No, tell him I'll hear what he has to say, please!"

*　　*　　*

When she quickly changed out of her nightgown and came down into the parlor, a man in an expensive-looking suit was sitting on the sofa with a suitcase beside him.

"Well, well. Good evening. It's a pleasure to meet the young head of the Genoard family."

"No, I'm…nothing that impressive."

She didn't feel the position of family head suited her. She'd meant to yield it to Dallas as soon as she could, but Dallas had said that being the head of a ruined family was more trouble than it was worth, and he kept dodging the issue.

As a matter of fact, this was Dallas's way of being kind to his little sister; he wanted Eve to get the better part of the deal. Unfortunately, it was having the exact opposite of the effect he'd intended.

Eve knew nothing about her brother's clumsy consideration, and she simply answered that she wasn't suited to this. However, her guest shook his head. "No, you have a dignity that befits the head of a family. By rights, a lady like you shouldn't set foot in a casino run by mafiosi like the Runoratas, no matter what."

"You knew about my invitation?"

"I assumed they'd been sent to most of the affluent citizens in this area. I just happened to choose to call on the Genoard family… Or that's what I'd like to tell you. The truth is, I didn't think a young lady such as yourself would have any connections to professionals like me."

"…Professionals?"

Eve tilted her head, wondering what sort of professional he meant, and the man obliged her with an answer. "In gambling, of course. I'm a personal gambler."

"A personal…gambler?"

"I'm not surprised you've never heard of it. After all, I doubt you've ever had anything to do with casinos before. The wealthy who are accustomed to such places employ people like myself in order to win efficiently, or to make gambling more enjoyable."

The guest took a pack of cards from the pocket of his tuxedo, slid them out of their box, and shuffled them dexterously. Taking cards in his left hand, he warped them in his fingers and forcefully "fired" them. It was a type of shuffling commonly referred to as the "riffle shuffle." Since it tended to damage the cards, it wasn't ordinarily considered a good method.

However, Eve had only ever used cards during card games, and to her, that fancy technique looked like magic.

The guest executed a different type of showy shuffle for the startled girl. "...I'd imagine you don't feel you need a professional like me. You may not even plan to visit a casino. However, I haven't come to beg you to hire my skills." At that point, the guest stopped shuffling, and he placed his suitcase on the table. "That enormous casino the Runoratas are hosting is going to attract all kinds of dealers. Others in my line of work as well, of course. I simply want to test my skills there!"

Speaking more forcefully, he opened the suitcase. It was filled with bundled bills.

"I'll pay for the chips on the day. If I manage to win, I'll give you the full amount. If I lose, then that's it, but... Please. Would you let me attend that party as your companion?"

The man held out a bundle to Eve. "I haven't introduced myself yet. My name is Nader Schasschule. In exchange for this, please sell me the right to escort you at the casino."

After he'd said it, Nader felt a nasty sweat break out on his back. *Am I an idiot?*

A professional gambler? Even a kid wouldn't buy that line! "Please sell me the right to escort you"? *What the hell was that?! You're not propositioning a hooker, pal.*

Even as he mentally cursed at himself, he didn't let any of it show on his face or in his gestures.

What was a guy who'd been lying low at a lodging house doing in a place like this?

It was all due to his cowardice.

⇔

Five hours earlier   The first floor of the lodging house

Once Ladd and the others had left, the lodging house was quiet.

"What was that all about, huh?" Roy was relieved the storm had passed, but Nader was shaking in his shoes.

What is this…? Seriously, what's happening? What kind of current am I swimming in?

Do I have any advantage here? Do I have any kind of shot at crushing Huey's organization?

The current, right… I have to figure out this current.

Figure out the current—it was a weird way to put it, but really, he was just looking for an excuse to cut and run.

It was a trick Nader used frequently when he needed to duck an important decision.

He'd tell himself that if he threw the die and got a one, luck was going his way, so he'd bet big. At first glance, that seemed optimistic, but it was a gamble he'd lose five times out of six.

In other words, five times in six, he could say, "Oh, I didn't get it, so I guess that's that," and give up. Even if he did happen to throw a one, he'd just look for another reason. "If I don't get rained on before nightfall," "If I win three games of solitaire in a row," "If I throw a rock so it goes right by that dog over there, and he doesn't bark"… He'd bet on all sorts of different things, and when he lost these bets, he'd tell himself, *Today's a bad day for it*, and give up.

He could ride this current, march into the Runorata casino, and crush Huey's organization. Then he'd return to his childhood friend, boldly and triumphantly, as a hero. That future seemed ridiculous, but if he denied it without even giving it a shot, he didn't think he'd be able to look either his childhood friend or his past self in the face. Even if assuming he could ever do that again was pretty presumptuous, he knew.

However, to convince his wishy-washy self, he decided to give it a shot.

To make it easy to give up, he set a goal that was just this side of impossible.

*   *   *

If I manage to trick one of the rich folks who got an invitation and sneak into the Runorata casino event, then I'll charge straight through to the end. Even if it means risking my life.

It was a completely crazy bet.

It obviously wasn't going to happen.

In the first place, he had no connection to any of the wealthy families in the East. He didn't know which of them had connections to the Runoratas, and besides, who would listen to some guy they didn't know from Adam in the middle of a recession this bad?

If a current that was to his advantage had really flowed in, it would carry him through those hardships, and everything would go smoothly. All day today, he'd look for rich people while steering clear of Hilton. If it didn't work, he'd let it go.

Nader felt like a coward for giving himself a built-in escape route, but he didn't have the courage to go against his own nature.

There was one problem, though; there was something he'd failed to notice.

The current he thought he'd stopped just short of had actually swallowed him long ago. It had probably happened back when he was with Huey, the moment he learned about the immortals.

"Hey, Roy. You wouldn't know of any rich folks who might have ties to the Runorata Family, would you?"

There was no way a former junkie and assistant lodging house manager would have rich friends. He'd asked as an easy first step in his search, but he didn't get the answer he was anticipating.

"Hmm? Oh… Yeah, technically."

"……Huh?"

"Her name's Eve Genoard. That family's got all sorts of close connections to the Runoratas."

"Y-you aren't gonna tell me you know where she lives, are you?" Nader asked timidly.

Roy shook his head apologetically. "Nah, I'm afraid I don't know that much. I do know it's somewhere in New Jersey."

"I see. Yeah, that makes sense."

Vaguely relieved, Nader tried to wrap things up quickly, but somebody ambushed him out of left field, breaking into the conversation.

"What, Miss Genoard's place? We know where that is. Right, Miria?"

It was the pair of odd ducks Fred had introduced as his new cargo movers.

"Yes, Isaac! We went to case the joint lots of times, so I remember it really well!"

⇔

In the parlor at the Genoard residence

And now, in the present…

He'd been concerned by that expression Miria had used, "case the joint," but before he'd figured out what to do, he'd found himself sitting in front of the girl in question.

He'd said he didn't want to go into town because it was dangerous. However, Graham had offered to have Shaft drive him over, and so here he was.

He'd told the butler, "I have a proposal regarding the Runorata casino," but he'd never dreamed the Genoards had actually received an invitation.

The coincidences had to end here, though.

Not many would believe a story as fishy as his.

They'd have to be either terribly hard up or incredibly dim.

After all, he'd ignored all the methods he would have used to pull off a con and winged it, ad-libbing recklessly. The only thing he'd done by way of psychological manipulation was intimidate her by shuffling cards.

Now Eve would get mad at him—"*You shady grifter, what's your game?*"—and that would be the end of it. He'd just have to give up gracefully and beat a retreat before she called the cops. That was what he figured would happen, at least.

"...All right. I do have some conditions."
Eve's voice was more serious and earnest than he'd anticipated.
"......Huh?"
Nader sounded dubious, but the girl stated her terms anyway.
"I don't need the money. In exchange, I want you to help me persuade my brother to let me take him home."

In that moment, Nader finally caught on.
This wasn't just a current. He'd already stepped into an enormous maelstrom.
And just now, he'd been dragged firmly into the new whirlpool this girl, Eve Genoard, had created.

The vortex that surrounded the immortals was growing more turbulent.
It absorbed several other whirlpools, large and small, that had been generated by the mafia, the Camorra, and various individuals.
No one knew what lurked in the darkness below that torrent yet.

Nader Schasschule kept sinking toward that blackness. He couldn't fight the current. He couldn't even make a small whirlpool of his own. He could only sink deeper into the cold, deep darkness.
Unlike the others, he couldn't even harbor a little desire that would work in his favor.

Linking Chapter   Nobody Can Throw Stones

A port somewhere on the east coast of America

Several hours had passed since Victor's visit to Edward. Evening had arrived.

"Hey! Whaddaya mean, 'We can't check into it'?" Victor barked.

He'd had his men investigate the direction the seaplanes had flown in after the previous day's attack on New York, and he had hit on the possibility that their main base might be moving somewhere out on the ocean.

After narrowing the options to a few ports that seemed likely to be on their supply route, they'd checked into the ships that had entered and left. In one port, they'd discovered vessels that had kept their departure data and their cargo under wraps. Sure he'd found a winner, Victor had gone over there in person, but they refused to issue a warrant that would let him search the boats without needing consent.

Out on the wharf, in the blustering wind, Bill Sullivan faced his livid superior and scratched his cheek, looking embarrassed. "Uh… The thing is, they're foreign ships. There were issues."

"There are idiots who were blazing away over New York with machine guns on those boats! Even if they were firing blanks, this is no time to hold back just because they ain't from here!"

"Well… They aren't just 'not from here'… Erm, they've got a bit of a connection to our department, so I think we should tread carefully."

"Huh?" Victor sounded dubious.

Bill handed him a pair of binoculars and pointed to a vessel that was out at sea. "One of those ships just left port a few minutes ago, and it's lying at anchor offshore. I think it'll be faster if you take a look for yourself."

"Quit beating around the bush. It would obviously be faster if you told me. They say a picture's worth a thousand words, but a good report sums up a thousand pictures *in* a word…"

Grumbling to himself, Victor looked at the ship through the binoculars.

He froze in an instant. Instead of grousing at his subordinate, he groaned in shock.

"You've gotta be kidding me…"

⇔

Night   The restaurant Alveare

"You got attacked, too, Maiza?!"

Since the police had questioned Maiza about the smoke screen, he hadn't made it to the restaurant until that evening. Firo had been surprised upon hearing the story, but his surprise had promptly turned to anger. "Dammit, Melvi again!" he snarled. "That son of a bitch is making monkeys of us."

"We aren't certain he's the one who did it yet."

"But I can't think of anybody else who would, can you?!"

"Even so, shouting before we have proof would be playing right into our opponent's hands."

Even though Maiza had been personally attacked, he was keeping his cool, and watching him made Firo realize just how far he still had to go.

I've gotta learn how to keep my emotions on a tighter leash, he thought, and tried to make some levelheaded conjectures about the situation as a whole.

However, after about ten minutes, he was forced to stop.

"Firo, telephone for you," Seina called.

"For me?"

Firo went to the phone at the back of the restaurant and picked up the receiver. "Hello? Firo Prochainezo speaking."

The voice that answered was a familiar one. *"Hello there, Firo. How have you been?"*

"Melvi… It's you, isn't it?!"

"Oh, you recognized my voice! I'm terribly honored. And? Are Yaguruma and Maiza also well?"

Melvi specifically naming the two who'd been attacked that day was an obvious taunt, and Firo almost blew a fuse then and there. But Maiza was right; if he lost his temper now, he'd be playing into his enemy's hands. He reined himself in before he answered so that the fury in his voice was buried deep.

"You don't have to explain a thing. Just start thinking about what corner of the ocean floor you'd like to spend eternity. And any snacks you'd like us to pack in the concrete with you."

"Well, well. You aren't threatening to eat me?"

"You're not worth it."

"Oh dear. You see, there's that personal bet I made with you… Since I want Szilard's knowledge, which is inside you, I thought I'd have to let you eat me if I lost."

There was a nasty, chuckling sneer in Melvi's words, and Firo's anger was boiling up again. As he responded, his voice trembled. "I see. Yeah, that damn Szilard's memories and your brains might balance the scales."

"Indeed. Still, I worried that might be too dull…" Melvi let a brief silence fall between them, then made an odd comment. *"Firo Prochainezo, it should happen any minute now. Don't hang up, all right?"*

"Any minute now? What are you talking about?"

Suddenly, the restaurant's door burst open. Czeslaw Meyer dashed through in ragged clothes.

"Czes?!" Firo almost ran over to him, but the voice from the phone kept him where he was.

"Don't hang up! Stay right where you are, Firo. Don't move an inch."

His courteous tone was gone; Melvi was speaking forcefully now. However, that unpleasant sneer was still there.

Both Seina and Maiza called to Czes, but he ran right over to Firo. "I'm sorry… Firo, I'm really sorry…"

"Czes…? What? What happened?!" Even as Firo spoke, he kept the receiver pressed to his ear. The reason he hadn't ignored Melvi and hung up was because the sight of Czes had made his blood run cold.

And his fear was absolutely justified in the worst possible way.

"The apartment blew up all of a sudden…and Ennis… Some strange men took Ennis…"

Firo's mind went white, perfectly blank.

In a sense, his way of escaping the reality.

The silence lasted only about a second, but to Firo, it felt like hours before roaring laughter came through the phone to shatter it.

"Ha-ha-ha-ha-ha-ha-ha-ha-ha-ha-ha-ha-ha-ha-ha! Ha-ha-ha-ha-ha-ha-ha-ha-ha-ha! Bingo! It looks like I managed to call at the best possible time! I'm so glad, Firo Prochainezo!"

There was no longer any trace of the politeness Melvi had shown when they met the previous day. He spoke loudly and cheerfully, like a kid crowing about a successful prank, while Firo wordlessly listened.

"All right, now our wagers are evenly balanced! If you win, I'll return Ennis to you unharmed! If I win, I'll take all of Szilard's knowledge from you. You know what that means, don't you? Well, if you want to cheat, you could cobble together a homunculus, use your left hand to share some knowledge with it, then give it to me. That would be easy if you used Szilard's knowledge, wouldn't it?" Melvi snorted. *"If you can make it happen by the time the casino opens, that is."*

"Hey... Wait..."

Firo's thoughts were just beginning to return to reality, and it took everything he had to squeeze out those two words.

Melvi went on mercilessly. *"Don't worry! I have no intention of eating Ennis! Although if someone were to do something stupid...like going to that newspaper, say, or the police...I can't guarantee the outcome. Even if I didn't eat her—because I didn't eat her—she might just suffer pain and humiliation for eternity. Ha-ha-ha-ha-ha!"*

It was a coarse laugh full of hatred.

Firo didn't understand where that bottomless hate was coming from. His voice trembling, he murmured, "...Why?"

He wanted to scream *Give Ennis back!* He wanted to tear Melvi apart.

However, his ties as a camorrista—the ties that bound him to his "family," the Martillo Family, just as they bound him to Ennis—managed to keep his emotions from breaking down entirely.

"Why do you hate me so much?" Firo asked. There was no need to ask how Melvi felt about him at this point.

The answer was easier, yet more incomprehensible, than he'd imagined.

"That's simple. Because you ate Szilard Quates." Melvi gave a short chuckle before his voice turned cold. *"You stole my future...and now you're going to give it back."*

"...Huh? What are you talking—?"

By the time he started to ask what that meant, the line had gone dead.

Still stunned, Firo looked around.

He could see Seina and Maiza, watching him with worry in their eyes.

Then he looked down and saw Czes. The boy's body was unscathed, but his clothes were scorched and burned through in many places, and the sight told him in no uncertain terms that this was real, and Ennis was gone.

And that was all Firo's rational mind could take.

*　　*　　*

Instead of screaming, Firo slammed a fist into the phone, shattering it.

He'd shattered his fist, too, but he didn't care. The phone was already in pieces on the floor.

Maybe it was because they'd gotten a look at his face, or maybe they'd figured out the situation from the way he was acting, but neither Seina nor Maiza said a word about the destruction.

Firo felt enough blame in the silence.

He should have run straight back to Ennis as soon as he'd heard that Yaguruma had been attacked. What a fool he'd been.

⇔

The Runorata villa　　Melvi's room

"All right… Now *I just need to nail down the demon.*"

After hanging up the phone, Melvi left his room. His expression was oddly cold.

As he started down the corridor, a voice called to him from behind.

"An exclusive phone line in your room? What magic did you use to make that happen?"

He turned around. A beauty with cold eyes was standing beside the door of his room. Her blond hair was pulled back, and she was wearing a casino dealer's uniform.

"…Carlotta. Eavesdropping? That isn't a very nice habit." Before he'd arrived, this woman had been the Runorata casino's top dealer. Melvi went on, still sarcastic. "Also, wearing those clothes outside a casino is in poor taste."

Carlotta narrowed her eyes slightly, but she didn't get angry. Her tone was indifferent. "Who you are is no concern of mine. That means what I wear is no concern of yours."

"If that's what you think, then tell your hangers-on to stop shadowing me."

"Tell them yourself. I'm not making them do that."

"Then what did you need? Don't tell me you've been lying in wait for me just so you could make sarcastic comments," Melvi baited her.

"Yes, just to be sarcastic. You're the one who'll be managing the new casino. Don Bartolo made that decision, and I wouldn't want to betray the Family by being jealous."

When Melvi heard that, he smirked. "...The Runorata higher-ups really are amazingly loyal to the don. Well, I'll do my level best to be useful to him as well."

"I see... In that case, let me give you one word of warning." Expression still cold, Carlotta narrowed her eyes again and murmured to Melvi, "Get a little *greedy*. If you don't, someone's going to knock your feet out from under you someday."

"Oh, come on. If you were listening in on that phone call, even if you didn't understand it, you must have noticed that I'm dripping with greed."

"...If that's genuinely an emotion you developed, then it isn't a problem." For the first time, Carlotta smiled faintly—and the smirk faded from Melvi's face. Turning her back on Melvi, she raised a hand, tossing a final remark behind her.

"I'll be praying that you notice your own true desire...*Melvi Dormentaire*."

⇔

Three hours previously   Somewhere on the east coast

Victor would never forget what he'd seen through the binoculars.

The distinctive family crest painted on the ship's side featured an hourglass.

It belonged to House Dormentaire.

*　　*　　*

It was a great noble family that had once employed Victor and Szilard as their personal alchemists, and they manipulated vast wealth as easily as if it were their own limbs. In the modern age, their power had waned, and he'd been aware they were only economically active in parts of Europe.

As a matter of fact, he hadn't heard a single scrap of information that the family was involved with the American immortals incident.

"Why are they showing up *now* of all times?"

Victor stood frozen. In contrast, the ship with the House Dormentaire crest kept rocking gently in the wavelets.

It was as if it were mocking Victor—
Or this country. Or the world itself.

AFTERWORD

Hello, and congratulations on getting this far. This is Narita.

…And that was the second *1935* volume.

In terms of "beginning, middle, and end," this is still technically the beginning. I'd planned to include everything up to this point in the first volume, but due to page constraints, it ended up being two volumes. I'm very sorry about that… That said, while it may have been the beginning, in terms of the "introduction, development, twist, conclusion" structure, it covers everything up to "development."

In the next installment, we'll finally transition to the casino event, the "middle" and/or "twist" section. But first, there's going to be a *Baccano!* side story volume, similar to *1932 Summer*.

Also like that volume, it's an expanded version of the second half of the bonus novels that came with the anime DVDs.

I think opinions about this will probably vary. My personal opinion is that turning DVD bonuses into novels is similar to having a movie that's gone to DVD shown on TV for free; since it's been a few years, I hope you'll forgive my turning it into content again.

Of course, if it's not necessary, then there's no need to turn these things into novels. However, there's one big reason for turning this particular story into a book: An important character who's going to come up starting in the next volume has already been portrayed very clearly in this bonus novel.

I hesitated over which method to use, but since the 1935 arc is a final settlement of accounts for the 1930s volumes, I want to include as many characters as possible. I've decided to reveal each character's story to as many people as I can, so they can enjoy this crazy ruckus to the max.

This is going to be one of the currents that flow toward the conclusion of *Baccano!*, so while I'm sure I'll get some criticism over this move, I hope you'll watch the series play out all the way to the end before you make your final decision on it.

After the side story volume is released, I'll fit in a volume of

DRRR!!, then head into *1935-C*... Or that's the plan anyway. However it works out, please continue to give all my series your support!

My tenth anniversary as a professional author is coming up, and while I'm delighted about that, I can also tell my stamina isn't what it used to be. Back when I made my debut, I could stay up for days on end; if I pull a single all-nighter now, I'm groggy and useless for two days afterward.

I guess I've gotten old. *Curse you, time...*is what I thought, but come to think of it, I haven't gotten any decent exercise since I became an author. The culprit wasn't time; it was lack of exercise. I pinned a heinous false charge on time, but I'd like to think it's because I'm getting older and my brain has started to rust. *Curse you, time...*(and repeat).

As for what I've been up to lately, as usual, except when I'm deeply on deadline, I've spent all my time gaming. I discovered there's an indoor airsoft field in my neighborhood, and I've joined games now and then, but even when I'm getting exercise, it still has to be kinda like gaming. I feel that games are the height of culture, and I'd like to keep improving so that I produce works of entertainment that can hold their own against these various games.

I got kind of serious at the end there because I realized, *Wait a second. I genuinely don't have anything to report except for the games I've played* and had to frantically cover my butt. In any case, in lieu of a report on what I've been up to, let's just say I have enough emotional leeway to game.

I managed to get my place cleaned up and had an air conditioner with a humidifier installed, so now I can relax and game...*koff, koff*...I mean, get cracking on my manuscript.

I suspect I'll be doing even more projects here and there next year, but I hope to go through the coming months and years with all my readers, and I'll be praying that all of you have a happy New Year's.

I hope to have your support in this next year as well...!

*The regular thank-yous start here.

To my supervising editor, Wada (Papio), and the rest of the Dengeki Bunko editorial department. To all the copy editors, for whom I always cause trouble by working too slowly, every single time. To the staff in all the departments at ASCII Media Works. This time around, things were already insanely busy due to the twentieth anniversary festival, and my late manuscript made things even crazier. I'm really sorry about that.

To the people who are constantly taking care of me: my family and friends, and other writers and illustrators.

To Director Omori, Ginyuu Shijin, and everyone else I'm indebted to in anime, manga, games, and other areas of the media mix.

To Katsumi Enami, who breathes life into the ever-expanding cast of characters in my fumbling attempts at novels, even while succeeding right and left at various other jobs.

And to everyone who read this book.

November 2012, Ryohgo Narita